RIVER
BOY

Books by
OLIVE PRICE

Three Golden Rivers
The Valley of the Dragon
The Story of Marco Polo
The Story of Clara Barton
The Glass Mountain
The Blue Harbor
Snifty
The Golden Wheel
River Boy

RIVER BOY

by Olive M. Price

Illustrations by
Bill Hamilton

Philadelphia
THE WESTMINSTER PRESS

Price, Olive M
    River boy.   Illus. by Bill Hamilton.
Philadelphia, Westminster Press [1959]
    176 p.   illus.   21 cm.

    1. Hudson Valley — Hist. — Revolution — Fiction.   I. Title.

PZ7.P9316Ri   813.54   59–5524‡

Library of Congress

*For Mary A. Mercer, lifelong friend
who opened the door to the world of books*

Contents

1

The Escape

Danny raised his spyglass like a pirate on a pirate ship.
Out toward the horizon he could see Atlantic white-
caps dashing in to mingle with the waters of Sheeps-
head Bay. He could see gulls winging toward this
south shore of Long Island, the sails of a frigate flying
the British flag in this year of 1777, the outline of a
lumber barge slowly making its way toward New York
harbor.

He could see these plainly, but nothing of his friend
Rob's rowboat. Once every week Rob came with his
father, who bought produce from the farms surround-
ing the little village where Danny lived with Widow
Reeves.

Where was Rob? fumed Danny. What was making
him so late? Had he run into a blockade suddenly
thrown up by the British? That hardly seemed likely.
There was no blockade now as there had been almost
a year ago during the dreadful Battle of Long Island.
The British had New York and from all that Danny
could hear the soldiers were enjoying their occupation

9

of the town as much as if they had been invited there for a party.

Danny adjusted his spyglass again but still he saw no sign of Rob rowing toward shore. The spyglass was a relic that he had found in Widow Reeves's tool shed. She had given it to Danny as something of little value, but to him it was among the greatest of his meager store of treasures. Next to the ship models he carved out of wood, the spyglass was the thing he cherished most.

He was poised high on the lookout he had built among the branches of a towering elm tree in the widow's garden. It had a strong wooden platform on which he was standing and a seat on which he could sit to whittle his ship models when he had time. A chore boy had precious little time for fun.

Danny was an orphan. He was grateful to Widow Reeves for taking him in, and he worked very hard for her. There were those who said that she would not have befriended him if she hadn't had a secret motive. She paid him nothing, of course. All he got for his constant service was food — poor food at that, grudgingly doled out to him — and the doubtful privilege of sleeping on a hard, narrow cot in the loft above the chimney corner.

" Danny, Danny! " He heard her call in a nagging voice from the kitchen. Danny shrugged. What, he wondered, what can she want now? Whatever it is, she can wait. I've got to see Rob.

He straightened himself up tall and again he ad-

justed his spyglass. The waters of the bay were bright
with May sunlight. Where they curved along the shore
they sang on sand rich with clam and oyster beds.
These were jealously guarded by sea gulls flying in to
feast upon them before sunning themselves on the
rocks at the water's edge. Often the gulls scolded the
sandpipers that sprinted along the sand. Danny listened to the cry of a herring gull. Then suddenly he
had ears and eyes for nothing but the sight of a rowboat that surely must be Rob's!

" Yo ho, Danny! " Across the sunny waters came the
sound of Rob's voice.

" Yo ho, Rob! " Danny called back to him with glee.

He took the spyglass down from his eyes and waited
impatiently while Rob kept rowing toward the shore.
Danny wanted to race down to meet him but he knew
if he did, Widow Reeves would be out of the house in
a flash with something for him to do.

So he waited, stretching himself so that he might see
every single move thirteen-year-old Rob was making.
Danny was even taller than Rob in spite of the fact
that they were both tall for their age. And he had the
strength of a young bull, the widow often said, and a
back as straight as an Indian's. His hair was bright, almost the color of copper, and his dark-blue eyes were
keen. His manners were alert, and he was smart as a
whip when it came to learning things, out of horn-
books or otherwise. People liked to see him smile.
The widow sometimes claimed that Danny Beckwith's
smile could charm the birds right out of the trees.

Nevertheless, she made him work like a slave. A boy's
hands with nothing to do, she claimed, could get him
into trouble fast.

Soon now, very soon, Rob would beach his boat and
come running toward the lookout. In no time at all he
would climb the tree, and then, as always, there would
be news from the world outside. A world exciting to
Danny. A world of ships coming and going. British
soldiers in bright-red coats — rebel Americans in rag-
gle-taggle costumes that could scarcely pass for uniforms. The world of gallant General George Washington fighting to win a war.

Danny felt a sudden thrill. Perhaps when a few
more months had passed, and he was then fourteen
years old, he could go away with Rob, never to return
here. He would take his ship models and his spyglass,
pack them up in a gunny sack. Once he had reached
New York Town — oh, but he had dreams! Wonderful dreams! He would work at things that had to do
with ships — anything, anywhere! Perhaps a frigate
manned with guns if the war was not yet over. Perhaps
a Dutch sloop or a tug, or even a flatboat or lumber
barge! Any kind of boat at all as long as it took to
water!

" Hey, you! " Rob was calling from the foot of the
tree.

Danny looked down at him, grinning.

Rob climbed up the tree like an acrobatic squirrel.
In less than a moment he was standing on the lookout,
face to face with Danny. Rob was a dark-haired, dark-
eyed lad, square of shoulder and just as lithe as Danny.

Danny saw at once that his friend had a queer look on his face. Something unusual had happened. Danny hoped the rebel army had not suffered another defeat.

" Danny," Rob began, and his voice was sober.

" Well? " urged Danny, then after another second of silence, " well, what are you staring at? Seeing a ghost? "

Rob looked at Danny a moment longer. His eyes seemed to be measuring his friend as though he was judging Danny's size for the first time, then he burst out,

" You've got to get out of here! "

Danny stared back at him.

" Out of where? "

" Out of here," repeated Rob. " Away from Widow Reeves."

" Why? " snapped Danny, now really surprised. " Are the redcoats on the march again? "

" It's not the redcoats. It's the widow."

" The widow? " echoed Danny.

Rob nodded vigorously.

" If you don't leave here tonight, you're lost. She's going to sell you tomorrow morning."

Danny's cheeks flamed.

" Sell me! " he cried. " I'm not a slave! "

Rob laid his hand on Danny's shoulder.

" She's got some kind of right because she took you in as chore boy. Father and I just heard the news from Farmer Jeremiah Gray. We stopped to buy eggs and chickens, and he told Father all about it."

" Farmer Jeremiah Gray! " Danny almost shook

with scorn as Rob paused. " Everybody knows that he's an old weasel! "

Rob looked grim.

" Sure, he's a weasel," he agreed, " but still he wants to buy you and the widow says she'll sell your services. He's going to give her so many pounds in cash tomorrow and the rest of it when you're twenty-one. That will make you his bound boy for the next seven years."

Danny felt suddenly sick at his stomach. So those people had been right when they had said the widow had a motive for giving him a home.

" I'll never be a bound boy! " he roared. " The widow is a traitor! "

Rob shook his head, agreeing.

" That's what I told Father. Anyhow, Farmer Gray's coming to get you early tomorrow morning."

Danny backed away from Rob, his face as white as chalk.

" I'll have to run away," he said. " Now. Right now."

" But you can't run away in broad daylight," Rob said. " They'll capture you for sure. You'll have to wait until after dark."

Danny sat down on the seat built in the corner of the lookout, and cupped his chin in his hands. He sat there brooding while Rob stood loyally by.

"You're right," Danny said. "I'll have to wait until after dark." Suddenly he leaped to his feet and faced Rob excitedly. " But I can't do that. I couldn't run far without them catching up with me. I have no horse and I have no boat." His eyes became very bright. " But you have a boat, Rob! "

Rob knew what Danny meant. Rob could take Danny back to Brooklyn. Once there it would be an easy thing for Danny to go on to New York Town and lose himself until he could decide what to do. Rob wanted to do this too but suddenly he knew he couldn't. What would his father say? Would his father be a party to Danny Beckwith's escape?

" Well? " Danny was questioning him anxiously.

Rob's shoulders sagged.

" Sure I have a boat," he said, " and I want to take you with me, Danny, but how about my father? Suppose he won't let me? "

Danny's face clouded.

" Your father is a good man," he said, " but I can see that he'd get into trouble if he'd help me get away." Danny got to his feet and began walking back and forth as if the lookout were a cage. " I'll have to find some other way."

Rob leaned against the tree trunk.

" We'll have to think hard," he said. " There isn't much time. Father will be waiting for me to pick him up at Farmer Gray's pier. We'll have the eggs and chickens ready to put into the boat — " Suddenly Rob yelled so loud and jumped so high he frightened Danny out of his wits. " I've got it! "

" Got what? " cried Danny.

Rob seized him by the shoulders, meanwhile jumping up and down. Finally he announced: "I've got the answer, Danny! You can be a stowaway! "

" A stowaway! " echoed Danny, entranced. " A stowaway on a rowboat? "

" Listen," said Rob, " we always carry big empty
crates. Some of them are big enough to put a live lamb
in. If you could hide yourself in one — cramp up
enough to fit — "

Danny was jubilant.

" Cramp to fit! " he repeated. " I'd sit cross-legged
and doubled up all across the Atlantic to keep from
being Farmer Gray's bound boy."

Rob roughly seized his arm.

" What are we waiting for? Let's go! "

" But I'll have to get my things," Danny protested.
" My ship models and my other shirt."

Rob was forthright.

" Walk right into the house and get them."

" That won't be easy." Danny smiled a wry smile.
" But I'll think of something to fool Widow Reeves."

" Good," said Rob; then he added, " I'll be waiting
in the boat."

Danny picked up his spyglass and handed it to Rob.

" You take care of this," he said. " I couldn't run
away without it."

" I know," said Rob, understanding.

The boys shinnied down the elm tree and looked
cautiously toward the house. There was not a sign of
life there. Only Lady, the Maltese cat, was stretched
out in the sun.

" Maybe's the widow's asleep," said Rob in a low
voice.

Danny wanted to laugh aloud.

" She never sleeps," he joked. " Always afraid she's missing something." He took a step or two on the path that led to the kitchen doorway. " I'll just go in as though nothing's happened."

" Be careful now," warned Rob, and turned back toward the water's edge.

When Danny entered the kitchen, the widow was standing at the table, mixing batter in a yellow bowl. She stopped beating with her big wooden spoon, looked at Danny, and scolded, " Didn't you hear me calling you? "

" Not exactly," said Danny.

She was thin and had thin lips, dark eyes that grew darker with fits of temper, and dark, straggling hair. Looks like a witch, sometimes, thought Danny, while she lashed out at him: " Laggard! Always a laggard! Go to the loft and fetch me your other shirt. I've got washing to do this morning."

That's fine, thought Danny, just fine. Now I know what I'll do.

He sprinted across the kitchen to the ladder that led up to the dingy quarters the widow called a loft, but he was whistling. He would put his shirt and a few other pieces of clothing he owned right into his gunny sack. His ship models were already piled neatly in a box of their own, and this would go into the gunny sack too. He would throw it over his shoulder and leave the loft by the one window, then he'd dash to the boat down through the garden.

Let Widow Reeves try to find him! Let her think of

how she'd planned to spend the money she'd expected to get tomorrow from Farmer Jeremiah Gray — the money she'd expected to get for Danny Beckwith!

Rob was waiting impatiently, his hands already on the oars when Danny raced down to the beach and tossed his gunny sack into the boat.

" We're off! " yelled Rob.

Inside the kitchen Widow Reeves stood at the foot of the ladder.

" Danny! Danny! Come down out of that loft or I'll take a switch to you! ".

Through the Dutch door behind her, two boys could be seen hastily rowing away from the shore.

Danny's hair was bright in the sun.

" We're pirates, Rob," laughed Danny. " Heave ho! We're bound for a far green isle! "

2

Stowaway!

The " far green isle " was Manhattan, but it was a long haul. The boys' destination was Brooklyn, and from there Danny counted on finding his own way to New York Town. Even though he had escaped from Widow Reeves, he was still in danger. How could he actually stow away on an open boat that had no cabin or companionway to hide in? This was still a problem the boys had to face in spite of those big empty boxes!

Rob had said they were in the rowboat — and there they were in plain sight of Danny, piled at the stern end of the boat. Some, as Rob had also said, were " big enough to put a live lamb in." True, he and his father had brought livestock to Brooklyn from farther out on Long Island, but Rob's father knew the extra load was there. Suppose Danny was in the box instead of a calf or a lamb? How soon would Rob's father become aware of the extra weight and try to find out what it was he was carrying?

After the first thrill of pulling away from Widow Reeves's shore line had passed, Danny faced this problem with growing anxiety. Once away from the sight of her house, he had crawled up on the seat beside Rob and taken an oar in his hands.

" We can make better time if both of us row," he was saying, but after a pause he spoke with sudden desperation. " But what's the use of making time? It won't work anyhow."

" What won't work? " asked Rob.

Danny explained what he had been thinking, that Rob's father would be sure to investigate the extra weight Danny made in the boat. Rob looked suddenly worried too.

" I never thought of that, but you're right."

Danny looked at the curving shore and added:

" It would be different if he didn't know that Farmer Gray wants to buy me and Widow Reeves intends to sell me in the morning."

And Rob reluctantly agreed.

" We just can't take the chance," Danny spoke again, discouraged. " Your father would have to turn me back to that old weasel of a farmer! "

He looked across the waters dancing in the sun, then resting on his oar for a moment, he reached down to the bottom of the boat and picked up the spyglass Rob had put there.

" What are you going to do? " asked Rob as Danny raised the glass to his eye.

Danny had spoken with bravado because he felt almost ready to cry. It had come as a sudden shock to him, the realization that this scheme of theirs could not really be put into action. Maybe, he thought now, I had better swim to Brooklyn! My chances of escape would be just as good.

Danny maintained a grim silence as he focused his glass first on the landward, then on the seaward side of the boat.

" What are you looking for? " asked Rob.

Danny took the spyglass down from his eye.

" I was looking for a boat," he said, " another boat to stow away on." Rob's face brightened as Danny went on. " There isn't a sail in sight — or even the sign of a barge — but maybe if we'd stay pretty close to shore, we'd find one anchored somewhere."

" A good idea," approved Rob. " If we could find another boat for you to hide on, we wouldn't have to worry."

" I'll never go back there! " cried Danny. " I'll never be bound to anyone! "

Rob nodded his head.

" We've just got to find another boat," he agreed.

Danny put his spyglass down, and both boys pulled hard on their oars.

For almost half an hour the boys rowed very hard. Sometimes they saw the distant sail of a broad-beamed Dutch sloop out toward the horizon. Once they saw the outlines of a British frigate in full sail, making knots toward New York harbor.

" We don't want a British boat," said Rob. " Your fate on that would be worse than a bound boy's. They say there's a filthy prison ship named *Jersey* lying in Wallabout Bay now. It's so terrible that men who are captured and taken to it have no hope of mercy. Somebody told my father — "

Danny grew taut as Rob paused.

" What did they tell your father? " he asked, seeing a shadow cross Rob's face.

" They said," began Rob, " well, they said that the prisoners are allowed to crawl around on the decks in the daylight, but most of them are so starved they can't even crawl. And at night when they are put behind bars the guards stick bayonets in them through the gratings."

Danny felt suddenly sick but he knew he had to hear such horrifying things. He was a boy on his own with no place to go. How else could he learn to escape a fate as bad or even worse if he couldn't plan to avoid it?

They were rowing close to the shore of a green cove. Just ahead, beyond the turn, lay the Narrows — a sparkling channel of water lying between the Brooklyn shore to the east and Staten Island to the west. A flock of gulls were flying toward low-lying hills on the island, now and then winging down to light upon the water and seize unwary fish. But Danny was not looking for gulls, much as they had always interested him. His eyes were searching the sandy crescent of beach that curved around the shore.

Suddenly he yelled: " Look! There's a boat! "

Rob stopped rowing and looked. Anchored not far from the beach lay a wooden craft built on the general lines of a Dutch sloop. It was larger than the usual river sloop, measuring, perhaps, fifteen by seventy feet, and could really be called a packet sloop. Someone had built a crude little cabin on its deck, which made it resemble a houseboat. Aside from this queer contraption, it was equipped with a mast set well forward, a small jib and topsail, and most wonderful of all, a big white sheet of canvas which was, of course, its mainsail, now bellying in the wind.

Its hull was painted red and its name was done in white. Suddenly Rob cried out in glee, " It's the *Mollie-O*, Danny! "

This meant little to Danny, for he had not lived near the harbor front all his life as Rob had.

" The *Mollie-O*," he echoed, looking ahead, pleased. There was something so jaunty about the way the boat sat on the water.

Rob was rattling on excitedly: " They say it once belonged to a pirate who sailed it as far as Trinidad but now it is only a store boat owned by Mollie O'Keefe. That's why it's called the *Mollie-O*."

" Mollie O'Keefe? " repeated Danny, puzzled. " You mean that it is owned by a woman — and — " he went on rather vaguely, " it's a store boat that — that sells things? "

Rob laughed aloud.

" You're getting the idea," he said. " Mollie sells things to women — hats and dresses and even fancy things like parasols. And for men she has knives and boots! In fact, she sells so many things Father says she has a corner on the market-boat trade."

" But where does she sell them? " asked Danny.

Again Rob laughed at Danny's rather blank expression.

" She sails up and down the Hudson River," he explained slowly. " She puts into port at all the little river towns from New York to Albany." Rob paused for a moment and frowned. " But what's she doing here in Long Island waters? There's no town or people to sell to. I've never known her to sail below New York harbor."

Danny was much more concerned with the boat than her present whereabouts.

" A woman," he marveled. " Is she the skipper? "

" Of course she's the skipper," answered Rob. " But she has a pilot whose name is Old Beaver. He's handled a tiller for so many years there's no one else on the river to match him. He knows the moon and the tides like you know the elm tree in the widow's garden. And he weathers those crazy thunderstorms up on the Tappan Zee that send other sloops to the bottom fast." Again Rob looked puzzled. " But what is the *Mollie-O* doing here — this far below the harbor? "

Danny almost stood up in the rowboat.

" I don't know and I don't care but that's the boat I'll stow away on. I'd like to meet Old Beaver."

Rob looked rather doubtful.

" If you could climb aboard her without being caught," he began.

Danny raised his spyglass and brought the *Mollie-O* in close range of his vision.

" She's got rope ladders," he announced, " hanging over her side."

Rob almost laughed.

" But you can't go up them in broad daylight without being seen by someone on board — and they'll haul the ladders in after dark."

Still looking through his glass, Danny spoke excit-

edly: " I can't see anyone on deck. Maybe if I try my
luck now —"

Rob looked startled. " Now? " he repeated. " Right
now? I'd be afraid to risk it."

Before he could go on, Danny seized his oar.

" Well, I'm not afraid," he said. " If I get caught,
I'll get caught. There's no one — not a soul — on
deck, and now's the time to take my chances. Let's row
over."

Realizing Danny was determined to try his luck at
any cost, Rob took up his oar from its resting place in
the oarlock.

" Don't say I didn't warn you," he began to scold.

But Danny looked sober and answered, " Don't talk
any more; just make time."

Swiftly and silently the boys skimmed across the water. Soon they reached the shadow of the *Mollie-O*.
Not until then did Danny speak again.

" There's no time for words now, Rob, but I want
you to know I am grateful for all that you've done. I'll
be seeing you again as soon as I can figure out a way —
and I'll never, never forget that you saved me from being sold as a bound boy."

Rob looked a little sheepish.

" Aw," he began, not accustomed to such emotion
from Danny.

" I mean it," said Danny briefly; then, looking up
at the sloop, he smiled. " We've come upon a right
gallant ship."

They maneuvered the rowboat until it was in a position from which Danny could grab the rope ladder.

He put the spyglass into his gunny sack and swung the sack over his shoulder. Then, quick as a bird off on the wing, he swung up onto the lower rung of the ladder.

He was so light and fast on his feet that Rob sat openmouthed watching him go up the ladder, which swayed a little under his weight. Rob even forgot to pull away at once to the shelter of trees overhanging the cove. He had planned to hide under their branches until he was sure that Danny had really stowed away and would not be thrown off the *Mollie-O*.

Meanwhile Danny's feet were swift and very sure. In no time at all he had reached the deck, turned and signaled to Rob that there was no one on it.

Odd, thought Rob, that's very odd, as Danny disappeared from his sight. I still wonder why Mollie's anchored here. She must know she's in what amounts to occupied waters and that British gunboats are masters here just as they are in New York harbor.

Picking up his oars at last, Rob still questioned the *Mollie-O*'s appearance here as he rowed away. It was a mystery — a downright mystery — that she should be anchored with no one on deck.

But Danny Beckwith was on deck now and he, for one, was exultant. For the first time in his life, even though he was in danger, he was walking the actual deck of a ship, feeling her sway with the tide. Even though he was in danger, his sea legs were being born!

A small boat lay on the *Mollie-O*'s deck. Danny hastened toward it. With eager fingers he unrolled the canvas that covered it and threw in his gunny sack. A moment later he too was in the boat, pulling the canvas back to cover him like a roof.

At that moment he heard a raucous voice squawking. " Wait for Mollie," it was crying. " Tell her I won't eat such swill! "

Then he heard a man's voice scold, " I'm the cook here, you rank bird! "

Danny suddenly smiled. The squawking had come from a parrot. There was a parrot aboard the *Mollie-O!*

Mollie herself, he reasoned, must have gone ashore.

3

Emalie and Tad

Again came the voice of the parrot, jeering: "Cook!
Cook! Ha! Ha! Ha!"

Danny almost laughed out loud. The parrot
sounded so human, so funny. Someone aboard must
have spent a lot of time training the bird to speak —
or had it really been smart enough to pick up a pe-
culiar lingo of its own?

He had heard many stories about parrots being
brought into New York Town by sailors. They found
these birds with shining green plumage and orange-
colored bills in South America. He wondered which
country this one had come from. Had the pirates who,
according to Rob, had once owned the *Mollie-O,* and
sailed her down to Trinidad, brought the parrot back
from the lands of tropical sun? Wherever it came from,
the bird sounded droll. He hoped that he might stay
aboard the *Mollie-O* and become its friend.

From what he had learned from Rob, Danny tried
to picture the people who lived on this boat and made
it their home. There was Mollie, of course, and Old
Beaver, the pilot, who as Rob had made clear had han-

dled a tiller for so many years there was no one else on the river to match him. Danny wondered what Old Beaver would look like — was just beginning to dream up a picture of the pilot in his mind when — wham! Something hit him square in the face. Simultaneously there was a cry, " You've thrown it in the boat! "

A girl's voice. A girl, thought Danny, instantly on his guard. The ball had rolled down under the canvas and lay like an apple on his chest. What should he do? he thought in panic. Should he sit up like a ghost — or —

He had no time to decide. Two young figures like wild Indians were throwing themselves into the boat, each scuffling hard to be the first to lay hands on the ball.

" Ouch! " yelled Danny taking the ball in his own hands.

He lifted the heavy canvas above him and stood up so suddenly that the girl was taut with surprise. The boy beside her exclaimed, " It's a stowaway! "

Danny stepped out of the boat with all the dignity he could muster. He found himself facing a long-legged girl, perhaps twelve or thirteen years old. She looked more like a boy than a girl because she wore blue sailor's pants. Her hair was tucked under a sailor hat, and her pretty blue eyes, now that she saw he was only a boy, were not really unfriendly.

The boy was more sober and looked a bit slouchy. His hair was a nondescript shade of brown; his eyes were brown too, almost matching the freckles that dotted his face like clown spots. He was as skinny as a

corkscrew, " no meat on him " Widow Reeves would
have said. His voice was an inquisitive drawl.

" Where'd you come from? " he questioned, staring
at Danny hard.

" What's your name? " piped up the girl.

Danny's hands were clenched into fists. One held the
ball they had thrown into the boat, but he released
the ball now, throwing it toward the girl, slightly on a
curve.

" Catch! " he said with a sudden bright smile, then
as she caught it, seemingly without effort, he added,
" Not a bad ball player, are you? "

" I'm very good," she bragged. " Better than most
boys."

" That's enough," the boy interrupted. " Never
mind the ball now. We asked him his name and where
he came from."

Danny almost smiled again. He realized that the boy
meant to act as though he was guarding the *Mollie-O*
— even trying to play boss — but somehow Danny
guessed that he was not really fitted for such a role
and didn't like it. This boy looked slow and easy —
mighty likable under his false pretense of the moment
— the kind who, as Widow Reeves might say, " would
rather go fishin' than let himself in for a lick of work."
Whoever he was, Danny surmised, he would make a
better friend than a halfhearted enemy, and if I'm
smart, thought Danny, I'll make all the friends I can.

He almost laughed out loud as the boy took a step
or two toward him, shuffling from one foot to another.

" You'd better tell me your name," the boy insisted.

Danny suddenly smiled his bright, warm, friendly smile. The boy blinked and looked incredulous as though he was being exposed to a sudden flash of light. Then Danny spoke.

"My name is Danny," he said. "I have to get to New York Town and don't have a shilling in my pocket. I aimed to stow away," he went on, "then when the boat got offshore to ask for work to pay for my passage."

The freckled-faced boy blinked again, and the tomboyish girl looked sympathetic.

"We haven't got a shilling either," the boy answered. "We live on this boat and work on it too. My name is Tad and this is Emalie, but we're no relation to each other."

The girl volunteered: "We are both war orphans; even our homes were burned when the British took over New York Town. Mollie found us on the water front with no place to go and gave us a home here on the boat. There's no one anywhere as wonderful as Mollie."

It was plain that they were accepting Danny as one of that forlorn company of boys and girls made homeless by the war. The fact that Danny was poor and had no place to go immediately made him one of them.

Danny explained: "I'm a war orphan too. My father was killed in the Battle of Long Island and my mother died soon after." Again he smiled at them both, not wishing to dwell upon unhappy memories. "Tad is a good name," he added.

Tad felt complimented. Danny's looks and bearing inevitably made people not only like him but respect him, and to homely, freckled-faced Tad, this boy had the air of a born leader. Somehow he felt drawn to

Danny and wanted Danny to like him too.

Emalie had the same reaction to this young stranger.

" Is my name good too? " she asked him almost hope-
fully.

Danny laughed. " Emalie," he said, then repeated
it slowly, " Emalie. It's a right pretty name, I think."

She kept holding on to the ball as she answered,
" Mollie thinks so too." She smiled as she added: " I
hope she lets you stay aboard. It's wonderful on the
Mollie-O. Even Tad is wonderful," she ended teas-
ingly, " only he's as slow as a snail."

Tad made a wry face.

" Thanks," he said pointedly, then he turned to
Danny. " Girls make me tired."

Again Danny laughed.

" I've never been around one," he told them. " I
never had a sister or brother."

Emalie sighed.

" That makes us three," she said sadly, " and I wish
these redcoats would pick up their guns and go home."

" We'll make them one of these days," said Danny.

Tad looked across the deck toward the shore.

" We'd better get out of these waters fast or they'll
come along in a frigate and turn their guns on us because we're here. Wish Mollie and Old Beaver would
get back."

So I was right, thought Danny. They are ashore as I
thought when I came on board and stowed away. Suddenly he asked, " What is the *Mollie-O* doing here? "

Tad and Emalie looked at each other.

" Shall we tell him? " she asked, a bit uncertainly.

" Sure," said Tad easily; then added, " Shucks, he's all right."

Emalie smiled.

" Reckon he is, and I'll tell him," she went on importantly, nodding toward shore. " There's a detachment of American soldiers hiding out in those woods to do what they call scouting, which is just the same as spying, I guess. Anyhow, they're trying to get a line on British movements here for General George Washington. The captain is Captain Johnny."

Tad interrupted as she paused: " Captain Johnny is Mollie's brother. She risked going ashore to take some good food to him and his men. She says young soldiers are always hungry. Old Beaver went with her."

Danny looked impressed.

" That's a risk," he agreed. " I hope she comes back soon."

Emalie spoke with full confidence.

" Mollie'll get back all right," she said. " Mollie can do anything." Suddenly she turned to Danny, asking, " Aren't you hungry? "

Danny was tempted to rub his stomach as Rob so often did but instead he smiled and said, " Hungry as a bear! "

Emalie's eyes sparkled.

" Let's raid the biscuit barrel! Last one to make it is a beggar and a fool! "

She turned away from them quickly and raced toward a barrel standing halfway down the deck at the top of the companionway.

" Girls," said Tad, looking at Danny disgusted.

" Let's go! " laughed Danny, taking after Emalie.

The barrel was big and plump and had iron staves around it. When Danny reached it Emalie was already lifting the lid and he saw that it was filled with cakes. Lemon and ginger, Emalie enlightened him.

" Take a handful," she said brightly.

" A handful! " he echoed, then grinned. " I've been taught better manners."

" So have I," she laughed, as Tad finally shuffled toward them, " but I don't always use them."

" I never saw so many biscuits," Danny said, amazed. " A barrelful — a whole big barrelful! "

Emalie reached into the barrel and brought forth a big handful. The lemon biscuits were yellow. The ginger ones were brown. Meanwhile, she stared at Danny blankly.

" Don't you know the *Mollie-O*'s a store boat? " she asked in surprise.

" So I've heard," he answered, " but I didn't know you sold biscuits and good things to eat! "

He took the cakes Emalie offered while she went on chattering: " We don't sell many things to eat, but William, the cook, makes these from a very special recipe he got down in the Caribbean. He says a cook in Port-au-Prince gave it to him."

Caribbean . . . Port-au-Prince . . . Danny's eyes had an enchanted, faraway look as Emalie spoke. You couldn't tell him that living on shipboard was not the most exciting life in the world! He just had to make a good impression aboard the *Mollie-O* so they'd let him stay! Emalie was still staring at him curiously.

" Well," she demanded, " why don't you try them? I thought you were as hungry as a bear? "

" I was, and I am," laughed Danny, " but you were just saying such wonderful things."

" Wonderful? "

Again Danny smiled, but there was almost a throb in his voice.

" I guess you're used to the names of faraway places like Port-au-Prince in the Caribbean, but to me they're just like a call." He couldn't help adding, " Someday I'm going to sail to every port in the world! "

" You hope," said Tad, jeering a little. " Speaking of calls, listen to this — "

As Danny bit into a ginger biscuit, Tad walked to the barrel and rattled the wooden lid. He and Emalie both cocked their heads and listened.

" Thief! Thief! There's the thief! "

Danny laughed out loud.

" Is that the parrot who was scolding the cook when I came on board? "

" That's Jinx, all right," laughed Tad. " He's the uncanniest, orneriest bird you ever saw. He can talk and he can hear and he can even smell things a whole mile away! " Tad paused to listen again as another raucous cry came up from below. " Lemon and ginger! Lemon and ginger! They're stealin' the biscuits! "

Emalie reached toward the barrel again.

" We'd better take 'em and run! " she suggested. " That pesky parrot catches on every time we rattle that lid! "

Tad was already moving off.

" Let's watch for Mollie and Old Beaver," he said, looking back.

" Let's! " cried Emalie, reaching for more biscuits with greedy hands.

" Thief! Thief! Thief! " Jinx was crying again as Emalie put the lid back on top of the barrel and headed after Tad.

" Come on, Danny," she cried, " or the cook will catch you; then there will be trouble! "

Danny followed them, taking long strides. Once they reached the stern of the boat, they sat down on deck, leaning their backs against the little house. Danny turned to look at it curiously.

" This little house on deck," he said, " makes the *Mollie-O* look like a houseboat."

Emalie smiled knowingly.

" That's what Mollie says but she had this cabin built to serve as a cargo room so we don't have to carry things up and down the companionway every time we put into port."

" Mollie's very smart," Tad added, then his voice held sudden warmth. " She's the nicest — the very nicest — person in the whole world."

Emalie's voice was very warm too.

" She's an angel," she said soberly. " Just a sort of real down-to-earth angel."

Danny took another bite of his ginger biscuit.

" And what about Old Beaver? " he asked.

" Old Beaver! " they said simultaneously, looked at each other and laughed. " You wait and see."

Suddenly Tad looked toward the woods beyond the white sandy beach.

"Guess you won't have to wait long," he said. "Here they come now."

Danny looked toward the shore too. He saw Mollie, a big, buxom woman, making her way toward the shore line. Then he saw Old Beaver and spoke with a sudden thrill.

"So that's Old Beaver," he said, surprised. "All dressed up in a red shirt, and his white beard looks a yard long!"

"Right!" said Emalie, laughing.

"Right!" added Tad. "And don't think his temper isn't as red as his shirt! And he's plenty tough on stow-aways!"

4

Mollie and Old Beaver

Tad ran to let down the Mollie-O's *gangplank, but*
Mollie called up to him: "Never mind the plank,
Tad. We'll climb up the ladder."

To Danny's utter amazement she paused for a moment on shore, slipped off a wide skirt with flowered
panniers, and stood ready to climb in blue sailor's
pants such as Emalie was wearing.

Emalie laughed at the blank expression on Danny's
face.

"Hope you're not shocked," she said gaily. "Mollie
always wears pants on shipboard. When she goes
visiting, though, she's very proper."

"Well, I guess pants are more practical here,"
drawled Danny and grinned.

When Mollie reached the deck and Danny saw her
face-to-face he was drawn by her motherly look of
kindliness. Some called her handsome, but that did not
wholly describe her in spite of her large dark eyes and
curly black hair streaked here and there with a bit of
gray. What really drew one toward her was her warm
Irish charm.

Then Mollie saw Danny standing on deck, question-

ing her with anxious eyes. One glimpse of this boy and
Mollie turned to Old Beaver exclaiming, " Sure an'
it's another one! "

Impulsive Emalie couldn't keep quiet.

" His name is Danny," she blurted out, " and he's
an orphan like me and Tad. He wants to get to New
York Town so he can work on a boat, but now that he's
seen the *Mollie-O* he'd like to work on it — like
us — "

Old Beaver interrupted and groaned, " Not so fast,
girl, not so fast! " Then he turned to Mollie. " There
you have the story an' he hasn't said a word."

Danny took a step forward and spoke a bit gravely,
" I haven't had a chance to speak for myself, but I'd
like to."

Mollie's voice was warm.

" Speak, Danny; I want you to. Emalie's such a magpie."

Before Danny could answer Old Beaver grumbled,
" She's another chatterin' female who can't learn to
wait until she's spoken to! " Then he too questioned
Danny. " How'd you come aboard, boy? "

Danny answered straightforwardly.

" As Emalie said, my name is Danny. My full name
is Danny Beckwith. My father was killed last year in
the Battle of Long Island, and my mother died a few
months ago." While Old Beaver kept looking at him
pointedly, Danny went on with pride. " I'm not afraid
to be on my own, sir, but I've just got to find work on
a boat. I've wanted to live on water ever since I can
remember."

"Huh," interrupted Old Beaver, not at all impressed. "All boys your age want to be pirates."

"I don't want to be a pirate, sir. I want to be a river boy!" For a moment Danny paused and smiled, then added, "I want to grow up to be expert like you."

"Bilge water!" Old Beaver roared. "You can't get on this boat by soft-soapin' me!"

" Beaver, you old bear! " Mollie immediately interrupted. " Don't frighten Danny before he starts. Sure
an' he looks a likely lad."

Old Beaver wheeled around to face her.

" You've already decided to take 'im on," he accused.

Motherly Mollie looked him straight in the eye.

" Sure an' I've decided," she said. " I am the captain
of this boat."

Again Old Beaver grumbled.

" I know you're the captain, Mollie, but you can't
take on every stray that comes along! This is just a
family sloop, and what with Emalie and that slow-
movin' Tad the family is big enough already! "

But Mollie looked unruffled.

" This boy has the makin's," she said very confidently.

" Makin's of what? " yelled Old Beaver.

" The makin's of a good river boy. I can see it in his
build. He's straight and tall, his hands look capable
and willing, and his eyes are as bright as a leprechaun's."

Danny was at a loss to know what a leprechaun was,
but had already surmised that Mollie was either from
Ireland or of Irish descent. Meanwhile Old Beaver
was storming: " You and your leprechauns! Can a leprechaun, I ask you, teach him how to change a mainsail? "

" No, but you can, Beaver." Mollie suddenly smiled.

Old Beaver stormed on. " Can your leprechauns

teach him what to do when the storm winds are
ablowin'? "

" No, but you can, Beaver," Mollie repeated, still
smiling.

" And what about a nor'easter? " he roared.

Mollie's voice was very gentle.

" You can teach him all about that too."

Old Beaver was about to roar again when Tad, who
had not said a single word since they had come aboard,
suddenly spoke: " I don't think you'll mind teaching
a boy like Danny, Old Beaver. He's not slow and shuffling like me."

Emalie, not able to be silent any longer, added,
" He'll make a wonderful river boy."

Old Beaver spat.

" You're all bewitched by leprechauns," he ranted,
then he turned to Danny. " You're on now — a river
boy on the *Mollie-O*. Mollie's the captain and she
wants it that way — but you won't like it, boy, I tell
you, you won't like it! Learnin' the ways of this river
is a man-sized job. By the time we reach the Tappan
Zee, I'll wager you'll want to get back on shore and live
the life of a landlubber."

Danny listened respectfully as Old Beaver went on.
Mollie listened respectfully too, but there was a slight
smile hovering around her lips. It was almost as though
she loved hearing Old Beaver rage. When he suddenly
stopped to catch his breath, she went toward him affectionately and laid her hand on his shoulder.

" Sure an' you're wound up like an old rusty clock,"

she accused him. " You'll love teachin' Danny the ways
of the river."

Danny too summoned the courage to speak to Old
Beaver.

" I'll be very grateful, sir," he said. " I'll work hard
to learn all that you can teach me."

Suddenly Old Beaver shook his shaggy white head.

" I'm stuck with you, boy," he said sulkily, " but
now that I am, you'll toe the line! "

Again Mollie smiled.

" He'll toe the line well," she said, " but now it's
time that the boy's gettin' settled." Turning to Danny,
she asked, " Did you bring any gear, Son? "

Danny looked guilty.

" I — I left it in the boat," he answered, " where I
stowed away."

Mollie ran her fingers through his bright hair.

" Go and get it," she said kindly. " You'll have to
share a cabin with Tad."

" I'd like that," said Danny forthrightly.

And Tad added quickly, " So will I! "

Emalie took off on a fast run along the deck.

" I'll get your gear for you! " she called back.

Old Beaver looked after her, scratching his head.

"That young interferin' female," he bellowed.
" Can't even let a man look to his own gear! "

Mollie laughed aloud as Tad started off with Danny
to follow Emalie.

" You just love women, Old Beaver," she told him
shrewdly. " If you didn't, it's one thing sure that you
couldn't get so mad at them." She laid a hand on his

arm as she added, " Now you go mind your helm, and I'll go down to see how the dinner's farin'. I think we're all hungry."

Old Beaver paused to ask as she turned away from him, " We'll be sailin' back with the sunset? "

" Right," answered Mollie. " 'Tis time we're getting out of these waters. Lucky we are we saw darlin' Johnny before a frigate came along to take a warnin' shot at us."

While Old Beaver sauntered off to see to the mainsail and take up his watch at the helm, Mollie disappeared down the steps of the companionway. As she did so she called to the young ones coming after her, " Bring all your gear down here and put it in Tad's cabin, Danny."

A few moments later, Danny followed Emalie and Tad down the steep companionway and along the narrow corridor that led to the ship's cabin aft. He had taken his gunny sack over his shoulder and walked along with such pride that he felt he would burst. So he was to be a river boy! One who would learn the devious ways of ebb tides and flood tides from the windswept deck of the *Mollie-O,* this gallant little packet sloop rigged with sails which he would learn to reef and change, depending on wind and weather.

Old Beaver would teach him well. And once he had conquered the river, then he would conquer the seven seas! He wished Rob were here on board with him — that they could talk about this high adventure as they had always talked in the tree house at Widow Reeves's.

" We'll be back in New York harbor by sundown,"

Emalie was babbling. " Have you ever seen the harbor, Danny? "

" No, I've never seen it."

Tad looked a bit envious.

" Wish I was seeing it for the first time again," he said dreamily. " There's nothing like the harbor at sunset. So many kinds of ships from ports all over the world — so many little river boats — sailing up and down. There are brigs and sloops and frigates — barges and shanty boats. Then there's British man-o'-war boats and their frigates manned with guns to take a shot at any ship that gets out of line."

Danny's eyes sparkled.

" It will be something special to see," he said.

Emalie spoke over his shoulder, " And just wait until we start up river." She faced him now with big, bright eyes. " When you see the Hudson River, Danny, Old Beaver will tell you that you are looking at one of the greatest rivers in the world. When we stop at port after port and you see the towns and the people — "

Tad slapped Emalie on the back.

" Listen, magpie," he scolded, " how about stopping to take a breath? I want to show Danny my cabin."

Enthusiastic Emalie looked quite unoffended.

" I want him to see the cabin too."

The door to it swung open on the portside of the *Mollie-O.* Danny's eyes beamed with delight as he had his first glimpse of a ship's cabin.

It was not an elaborate one, but it had bunks — upper and lower — and a round porthole from which he could see an expanse of blue water and shore line beyond. There were pegs on the wall for hanging up clothes; Tad's were already hung there, a curious array of blue sailor's pants and shirts and a yellow jacket. There was also a table with a blue china bowl and pitcher above which hung a hurricane lamp suspended on a chain from the ceiling. A mirror decorated one wall, and there was a shelf below it upon which was displayed an odd assortment of toilet articles, including a broken comb.

Danny's eyes took in the whole cabin with one happy glance.

" Wonderful! " he pronounced.

" It's pretty nice," admitted Tad, " and I'm glad you're here to share it. Throw down your gear on the bunk. You may have your choice of upper or lower — I don't care much where I sleep." He smiled his slow smile. " Sometimes I'm up and sometimes I'm down."

Emalie chirped: " Mollie doesn't care where he sleeps either — just so he keeps the cabin shipshape."

Danny threw his gunny sack on the lower bunk.

" Suits me," he said. " We can switch, if you like, any time you have a mind to."

Emalie was looking curiously at the gunny sack that bulged so awkwardly here and there.

"What are you carrying? " she asked inquisitively. " That sack bulges all over."

Danny laughed aloud.

" It bulges because it's so full," he said, and he picked up the sack, pulled at the drawstrings, and tumbled its contents out on the bunk. " You see, I like ships," he went on, enjoying the surprise lighting Emalie's eyes. " These are some I have whittled out of wood."

Tad was surprised too.

" Ship models! " he exclaimed. " They look great." Then he added, " And you've got a spyglass too! "

" My most treasured possessions! " laughed Danny.

Emalie took a ship model in her hands.

" It's even got a name," she began, then her voice was almost drowned by the clanging sound of a bell.

Danny looked inquiringly at Tad.

" That means it's time to eat," Tad told him, " and neither Old Beaver nor Mollie nor William, the cook, like to be kept waiting."

" Let's go then," said Danny, pausing, nevertheless, beside the washstand. " But I'd like to clean up a bit first."

" Me too," said Tad, " but we'll have to hurry."

Emalie laid the ship model reluctantly down on the bunk.

" I'll get out," she said, " but you'll have to show these to me later, Danny. When that bell rings a second time we've got to be at the table."

She hurried out of the cabin, closing the door behind her. Tad picked up the broken comb from the shelf.

" That Emalie," he said with mock scorn.

" But I guess she's pretty bright," Danny grinned.

" Just try to top her." Tad heaved an exaggerated sigh.

But as Danny washed his face and combed his hair one thing stood above all others in his mind. He was here in a ship's cabin. He was actually about to become a river boy!

5

The Harbor and the Town

Again the sound of the dinner bell. Tad threw his broken comb on the shelf and moved toward the cabin door.

"Time to eat," he said with a grin. "Hurry, Danny."

Danny gave his hair another quick lick with the comb he had unpacked from his gunny sack and followed Tad out into the corridor. Once they had arrived in the small cabin used solely for mess they found Mollie already seated at the head of the dining table and Old Beaver and Emalie in their places.

To Danny's utter surprise, Emalie had put on a clean white sailor's shirt. For the first time, he saw her hair — the color of tawny gold that added a deepening blue to her eyes. Then Danny suddenly blinked because he thought he was seeing things. Emalie, tomboy Emalie, had bound her hair with a bright-blue ribbon and looked very feminine indeed.

Mollie noticed his sudden surprise.

"It's Emalie, all right," she told Danny, laughing, "so don't stand there blinkin'. Believe me, Danny, she'd cut her golden curls just as short as your own hair, but I make her act like a lady at table — an' sure as you're born, she looks like one! "

Old Beaver was unfolding his napkin as Emalie put in a word, " I don't like wearing ribbons though."

Then Old Beaver growled, " Sit down, boys, and get to the business of eatin' your supper."

Danny and Tad sat down at the table. Mollie bowed her head and asked a blessing.

A moment later William stood in the entrance to the galley.

" You may serve now, William," she told him with a smile. " But say how-do-you-do to Danny first. The boy is to be one of us."

" How do you do, Danny," said William, a slight dark man with a narrow face. He added to his first greeting as he surveyed Danny with interest, " Welcome aboard the *Mollie-O*."

" Thank you, William," said Danny, " I am very proud to be here."

William, usually taciturn, smiled fleetingly.

" Spoken like a gentleman," he said, turning back to the galley.

Danny had eaten Long Island scallops but never as William prepared them. They had the taste of lemon and butter and the tang of bitter orange. Heaped on a plate with a mound of potatoes that looked as white as a saucer of snow, such food seemed to Danny fit for a king. Surely, he thought as he ate contentedly, some special kindly fate had saved him from being a bound boy and led him to the *Mollie-O*.

Mollie explained the shipboard routine. Tad's job, she enlightened Danny, was general chore boy to all on the boat, while Emalie was chore girl and salesgirl combined. He, Danny, of course would be apprenticed to Old Beaver but would be expected to help out whenever he was needed elsewhere.

" You'll be a busy boy, Danny Beckwith," Mollie went on. " And there'll be school lessons later."

Emalie turned up her nose.

" Lessons out of books," she scorned, " when we have the river to teach us! "

Danny disagreed with her gravely.

" I like lessons out of books," he said.

Old Beaver chuckled.

" Don't know when you'll have time for 'em, boy. When you're not tendin' sail or splicin' ropes you'll be learnin' the ways of navigation from river charts and manuals. An' you'll not be layin' a hand on the tiller for months an' months an' months. I don't believe in lettin' you handle a boat like the *Mollie-O* until you know what it's all about."

Danny looked disappointed, but Emalie spoke up brightly, " Studying won't be hard for Danny."

Old Beaver looked at her and grinned. " Oh, it won't, won't it? "

Emalie was not to be squelched.

" You ought to see the ship models that he's carved out of wood! "

" Ship models! " echoed Mollie.

Tad spoke up before Danny could. " He brought them in his gunny sack."

Mollie smiled warmly.

" Just like a true sailor lad. You'll have to show them to me, Danny."

" They're not much, really," Danny said, " although I'm proud of one or two. One is a Venetian galley I copied from a history book, and the other is a Norse long ship such as the Vikings sailed."

Mollie nodded vigorously.

" You see, Old Beaver? " she questioned. " What did I tell you? "

Old Beaver stood up and pushed his chair back against the paneled wall.

" What should I see, dear Mollie? " he sniffed.

This time her voice was sober. " That Danny Beckwith has the makin's."

Danny was emptying a tall glass of milk.

" Well, if he has so many makin's," Old Beaver drawled, " he can come and stand beside me at the helm while I take this old tub into New York harbor."

Instantly Mollie was on her feet.

" The *Mollie-O* an old tub! " she scolded. " Begone with you, Old Beaver, you old wind from the Tappan Zee! "

White-haired, white-bearded Beaver, who always enjoyed ruffling Mollie's Irish feathers, chuckled out loud as he left the cabin to go up on deck. As Danny hastened after him, Jinx, the parrot, chattered: " Time for Jinx now! Time for Jinx! "

Even the parrot, thought Danny amused, speaks out his piece on the *Mollie-O*.

Old Beaver had set the sails before supper, so now

he approached the side of the boat, calling to Danny over his shoulder.

" Do you know how to raise an anchor, boy? "

Danny hastened to his side.

" I think so," he said hesitantly.

" Well, it's very simple," said Old Beaver. " All you do is bring it up but you have to be careful not to foul it." He pulled on the anchor line with a jerk. " I took soundings of these waters before we anchored here, so we shouldn't have any trouble."

Danny watched Old Beaver's gestures.

" Bringing up the anchor looks easy," Danny observed, "after I see the way you do it."

" It's easy enough," Old Beaver said briefly. " Watch me now while I take the *Mollie-O* through the Narrows and into the harbor."

" Are the Narrows tricky to navigate? "

" Tricky enough," said Old Beaver, " especially when you're goin' against the tide."

Once through the Narrows, which lay between Brooklyn Town and Staten Island, Old Beaver headed straight for New York harbor. Danny was conscious of sea gulls following the *Mollie-O,* and when it passed a channel, which Old Beaver told him was the Kill van Kull, the sight of harbor traffic became so tempting that he could scarcely keep his eyes on what Old Beaver was doing.

Old Beaver grunted: " Take your eyes off me long enough to see what's goin' on, Danny. You can't learn sailin' all in the first run. It'll take months to make even a good cub out of you."

" Guess it will," Danny agreed.

He relaxed long enough to look around him while Old Beaver said: " Here's the big harbor, Danny. Hundreds of square miles of it."

" Hundreds of square miles! " echoed Danny, almost unbelieving.

" Sure is," went on Old Beaver. " An' that's a lot of water. Of course," he said wryly, " the harbor's not what it used to be since it's all fouled up with these British war boats. Over there on the East River they've got prison ships with our poor boys stuffed in the holds like rats." Old Beaver spat and nodded toward a British frigate now sailing by. " Look at that old buzzard! Guardin' these waters, she be, Danny, so our boats can't move without her evil eye on 'em! "

Danny breathed a long deep sigh.

Again Old Beaver spat as a British packet went by.

" Look at that rooster," he said with scorn. " We may have to take off our hats to British officers when we get on shore here an' submit to their raids and foraging parties, but I swear by all the river pirates that sail the Tappan Zee the *Mollie-O* won't bow to 'em on water! "

Danny suddenly laughed.

" There's scarcely room to bow," he said, " with all these boats coming and going. I never dreamed there would be so many, even in New York harbor."

" We'll find a berth," Old Beaver said confidently.

Danny watched while he maneuvered the *Mollie-O* toward the tip of Manhattan Island. Skillfully he threaded his way among barges and packets, frigates,

freighters, and sloops, and finally turned a bit westward toward the mouth of a wide river, announcing
to Danny: "There she be, boy, there she be! There's
the Hudson River stretchin' northward in front of
your eyes. It's a noble river, boy, and it'll talk to you,
that's certain."

"Talk to me?" asked Danny.

Old Beaver nodded.

"It'll tell you a story made up of things that happen
to you as you sail upon it. It'll be speakin' to you of its
waters aflowin' down to the deep sea, of mountains

above it like High Tor, where storms are brewed in witches' kettles, and of mountains where the Indians worship gods of the winds and the sky. It'll tell about the sailin' ships and the towns they sail to, but most of all it'll talk about the river people — good men and bad from the ends of the earth." Danny was charmed by Old Beaver's words and was just about to speak when the old man added: " You'll see the merchants of New York Town, the rebels, and the soldiers. You'll see river pirates on the Tappan Zee and Indian warriors runnin' all along the Storm King Trail. Hunters and trappers from Bear Mountain will tell you tales of the forest, and soldiers from West Point will mingle with signal men from Beacon. You may even hear a ghost up in the Catskills wailin' like a banshee — but all the time there'll be the river — deep and ever-flowin' back to the sea."

And thus Danny saw it — the Hudson River, magnificent now in the flaming aura of sunset, the mighty river that people said was really more than a river.

Tides and sea winds traveled with it more than a hundred miles north of this harbor, bringing the freshness of salt sea air to lush green meadows and towering mountains along its shores.

Old Beaver's talk had given wings to Danny's thoughts. He was now a river boy who would sail the Hudson up and down! He, Danny Beckwith, was destined to see its towns and people. What would he really see, he was wondering, and would he really be capable of meeting any challenge it might offer to him? Standing on deck, looking toward the river with exultant eyes, Danny felt as if he were like Henry Hudson seeing it for the first time on his voyage of discovery.

He was scarcely conscious of Emalie racing toward him.

" Look, Danny, look! " she called. " There it is! There's the Hudson! "

" You're late," growled Old Beaver. " I've already pointed it out to him."

Emalie answered blithely, " Well, I guess I can do it again! "

Tad came slowly up to Danny.

" It's a big sight, don't you think? " he drawled.

" A mighty big sight," Danny agreed.

Mollie came across the deck to join them.

" How's the wind for berthin', Old Beaver? " she asked.

" It's all right," he answered, " or will be when we reef our sails."

" I'll help," offered Tad.

" So will I," said Danny.

" There's a berth," said Mollie, pointing to a space between two freighters anchored at a slip on the westward tip of Manhattan. " It's a good one too."

Buildings loomed before Danny now — shops and stores and the red-brick homes of Dutch merchants. He could see crooked streets where wagons and carts rumbled. Here and there an occasional cow meandered along toward a lost meadow. British flags flew over the ramparts of buildings which Mollie told Danny were the stronghold of the British Army. Church steeples caught the glow of the sunset and gleamed like golden spires as they pointed skyward.

" It looks like a wonderful town," breathed Danny.

Mollie heard him and agreed.

" A wonderful town in peacetime but now it's full of shadows. We'll have to be careful tomorrow when we go ashore."

" Ashore? " repeated Danny, pleased. " Do you mean I'll get to see the town? "

Mollie laid her hand on his shoulder.

" You'll get to see it, Danny. I always do my buyin' here, so all of us take shore leave — even crochety Old Beaver! "

Emalie looked down at her feet.

" Are you going to buy me those slippers you threatened to, Mollie? " Her eyes were half beseeching.

" I'll be buyin' you slippers with bows, and you'll wear them in good company, Miss. You can't spend your life as a sailor lad when you've got golden curls and eyes as blue as the sky! "

Tad was glancing aft at the little cabin on deck.

" Our cargo room is almost empty, Mollie," he said. " You'll have to do a lot of buying if those snoopy British soldiers don't stop you."

" Spies, you mean, not soldiers," Mollie said contemptuously. " An' if they try to stop me, I'll find a way to smuggle what we need on board."

Danny listened to her wide-eyed. Mollie's empty cargo room. Buying things in New York Town under the redcoats' noses. Smuggling — yes, even smuggling! What an adventure he would be sharing!

His eyes were very bright as Old Beaver berthed the *Mollie-O*.

6

Danny and the Redcoats

The sky was still dark. Although the sun was not yet up, Danny lay awake. He missed the sound of roosters crowing, for he had always heard them at Widow Reeves's, but he could hear the wash of waters sloshing against the hull of the boat, and this was wonderful music!

Careful lest he should wake up Tad, still curled under his blanket in the upper bunk, Danny got to his knees. He crawled along the bedcovers to the porthole. Still kneeling, he stretched his neck to see what was going on in the harbor.

He was surprised to see that the British freighter that had been berthed next to the *Mollie-O* was gone. It had probably sailed with the early tide, and he wondered where it was bound for.

A faint glow heralding sunrise was lighting up the sky. Danny could see a narrow street meandering along the water front. Wagons and carts were already rumbling to the doors of various shops kept by Dutch and British merchants. He could even read some of the printed signs. One place was a ship chandler's shop.

Another sold silk and bamboo. Still another was a tavern. Hurry, hurry, he told himself — there are a thousand things to do!

He was up and dressed long before the bell rang for breakfast. Not even then did sleepy Tad stir.

"Hey! Get up!" Danny tugged at the blanket in which Tad was wrapped like an Indian papoose. "We have a big day ahead!"

Tad only turned over. "Go away, you early bird!" he muttered.

Still Danny tugged at the blanket. "If you don't get up," he scolded, "Old Beaver will come and get you! The breakfast bell rang long ago."

Tad jumped up like a jack-in-the-box.

"I didn't hear the bell!" he cried, swinging down from the upper bunk to the cabin floor.

Pulling on his pants, he hastened toward the wash bowl, adding, "You just don't dare be late for breakfast aboard the *Mollie-O*."

Minutes later they entered the cabin next to the galley. Old Beaver and Mollie were already seated at the table. William was pouring milk from a pewter pitcher while Jinx leered at them from his cage.

"Laggards! Laggards!" he cried. Then he cocked his shining head and cackled: "Where's that girl? Where's that girl?"

Emalie appeared in the doorway. "Here I am, you silly bird!" she called to him ungraciously.

Old Beaver muttered: "Mind your manners, will you, girl? The bird knows you're late."

Through all this hubbub Mollie sat serenely smil-

ing. She was accustomed to the moods of her " family "
at breakfast. She could be almost certain that Tad
would be a mite late and come shuffling in with one
eye on Old Beaver and the other on the eggs and ba-
con, that Emalie would arrive, happy in blue sailor
pants, without a frill or furbelow, that Old Beaver
would growl at the two of them while Jinx would chatter and scold. Then she would settle the lot of them
and outline her plans for the day. Breakfast was quite
merry on the *Mollie-O* — even to William, who never
failed to add to the uproar by banging his copper pots
and pans. And now that Danny was with them —
Mollie looked at him and smiled.

" Good mornin', Danny," she said. " An' how is it
that you slept your first night aboard? "

" Just like a log," he answered half shyly. " I don't
think I even dreamed."

With a sidelong glance at Old Beaver, she added:
" Sure, an' the leprechauns are carin' for you. They
know that if it's lessons you're to learn, it's sleep you'll
be needin'."

As she had expected, Old Beaver growled: " Leprechauns! Bilge water! The boy don't even know what a
leprechaun is! "

Danny looked from Old Beaver's scowling face to
Mollie's bright with smiles.

" I — I don't think I do," he confessed, half guiltily.

Mollie leaned forward.

" Well, now," she said, " I'll be tellin' you. Leprechauns, Danny, are fairies who take care of things in
Ireland. They have all the magic power of the little

people, an' when a son of Ireland needs them, I'm sure
they cross the sea to here."

" How big are they? " asked Danny.

Again Mollie smiled.

" Not big at all," she answered. " They're so little
they can stand up straight right on the palm of your
hand. They're always dressed in green and have whisk-
ers under their chins."

Danny tried to picture little men in green — so
little, in fact, that they could stand right on the palm
of your hand. With due respect to Mollie, all he could
really visualize were tiny human figures resembling
bright-green grasshoppers, but he had the grace to say,
" I'll be watching for them, Mollie."

" Good," she said, pleased. " Leprechauns will bring
you luck, but only if you believe in them. And now
all of you be listenin' while I tell you what we'll do today. Old Beaver," she questioned, " are you going to
the ship chandler's shop? "

Old Beaver nodded.

"I'll be goin' there first. We need ship's lanterns
and good strong hemp and bolts and bolts of sailcloth.
In these days sailcloth will be hard to come by this side
of the Tappan Zee."

Suddenly Mollie turned to Tad.

" Are you too sleepy to think of any gear we couldn't
be doin' without? "

Tad put down his glass of milk.

" I heard you say you wanted to lay in a stock of
hunting knives, Mollie. The kind the hunters and
trappers need up Bear Mountain way."

" Good," said Mollie. " I do."

Emalie pushed back her plate and turned to Mollie, saying: " We've got the list of things we must buy tacked on to the door of the cargo room, but I don't think we put patches and pomanders on it. All the belles upriver who flirt with the officers of the regiments ask for patches and pomanders as soon as we pull into port."

Mollie smiled, pleased. " I'm glad you remembered them."

Tad was smiling a wry smile. " What does Emalie know about flirtin'? " he teased.

Old Beaver complained: " Patches and pomanders, bilge water! Don't those belles upriver know we're fightin' a war? "

Mollie defended them stanchly.

" It's those do-nothin' belles who sometimes win a war, Old Beaver. An' if you be wantin' proof of it now, remember stylish Mrs. Robert Murray in her mansion on Murray Hill. Her charm captured the British general, Howe, so our General Putnam had time to escape with his soldiers. It was patches she wore on her pretty face, I'll be wagerin', and a pomander tucked in her fichu. So go along with you, Old Beaver, and give the devil his due! "

Old Beaver rose and pushed back his chair.

" Time for us to go along," he answered, " or we won't be ready to sail on tomorrow's tide."

Danny stood up a bit uncertain as to whom he should follow. Mollie laid an affectionate hand on his hair.

" You'll be goin' with Old Beaver, Danny. If it's a ship you will be sailin', it's time you start to learn what it takes to sail it by."

So while Emalie and Tad accompanied Mollie on her shopping tour, Danny went with Old Beaver. Once he set foot on Manhattan Island, he was entranced. The sights of the shops and the people gave him the feeling he was wandering through the pages of a book with pictures painted in vivid colors.

He could look back and see the ships in the harbor. More than any other the flag of England flew arrogantly from the mastheads of most of the ships in the big blue harbor.

" The British flag is everywhere," he said to Old Beaver, impressed.

And as always, when nettled, Old Beaver spat.

" We'll get a flag of our own," he said grimly, " and mind you, Danny, when that happens the *Mollie-O* will hang it so high on her masthead that even the British peacocks will have to stretch their necks to be lookin' up to it." He paused for a moment on the street, pointing a crooked finger at the New York populace. " Look at them strut among the people in their color-of-danger coats! "

Danny stood still to look at the passers-by. Mingled with British soldiers and officers were proud old Dutch merchants in wide pantaloons and broad-brimmed hats. Seamen in from ports all over the world looked jaunty in sailor's pants and caps. Negro slaves were at work in front of shops and houses while pretty ladies gracefully dismounted from carriages attended by

young gallants in uniform or foppish older gentlemen
wearing powdered wigs. How exciting this is! thought
Danny, then he turned from looking at people to
fasten his eyes on the shops.

There were rows and rows of them in New York
Town. Signs with pictures upon them to call attention
to the wares within were hung outside. A ship chandler's shop displayed a painted sailing vessel, a tailor's
shop a pair of scissors. A little black lamb hung on a
wool weaver's shop, and a golden key denoted a lock-
smith's. Taverns all had festive signs, such as: The
Silver Spoon, Fiddler's Harbor, The Golden Urn, and
The Big White Dish. Danny wished he could start at
the beginning of the street and take a peek into
them all.

" But now to business," Old Beaver was saying, and
turned in at a ship chandler's shop.

Once inside, Danny was all eyes and ears. The shop
had an odd musty smell and was filled with curious
things. Canvas and sailcloth. Miles and miles of rope
for riggings. Bowsprits and old anchors, and hundreds
of small things used in the building of a ship. Brass
bolts and rudder hardware. Caulking cotton and white
lead. Goosenecks for masts and booms. Bronze oarlocks. And there were wrought-iron lanterns and
weather vanes in great variety.

What intrigued Danny most was a collection of fig-
ureheads taken from old sailing ships. One was the
head of a youth with close-cropped curls like a Greek
god's. Another was a dolphin taken from a Danish
ship. Still another was the life-sized figure of a Viking

taken from a vessel from the Land of the Midnight
Sun.

He felt Old Beaver nudging him.

" Come, Danny," he said, " don't stand there dream-
in'. You'll call down a sailor's curse on yourself an'
never be able to live on land again if you let those fig-
ureheads beguile you! "

It took Old Beaver more than an hour to make the
many purchases for the *Mollie-O*. And whatever he
bought, he explained its ultimate use to Danny until
the boy felt his head throbbing with facts and figures
and all the items it took to make a ship complete.

When Old Beaver had bought all he came for, he
hired a wooden cart from the merchant so he and
Danny might take the things directly back to the
Mollie-O. Once it was packed and pushed out onto the
street, Old Beaver instructed,

" You trundle this back to the ship, boy, while I go
off on other business."

Danny started pushing the cart when suddenly he
heard his name being called excitedly: " Danny!
Danny! "

A moment later someone was pounding him on the
back, and he turned to see Rob. All in a moment his
thoughts took wings to the house of Widow Reeves
from which Rob had helped him escape the fate of
being sold as a bound boy.

" Rob! " cried Danny. " Am I glad to see you! "

" Me too," cried Rob, then fastened his eyes on the
cart. " How are you? What are you doing with all
this? "

" One thing at a time," laughed Danny, as he pushed the cart against the wall of a nearby tavern. " Let's sit on this wall and talk."

"Did you get to stay on the *Mollie-O?*" Rob was asking eagerly. "I just can't wait to hear. Tell me everything! "

They sat cross-legged on the wall, so absorbed in what each had to tell that they were scarcely conscious they were on a crowded street. While merchants and sailors and soldiers passed by, they talked on and on.

" Wish I could be a river boy," Rob was saying enviously. " Especially on the *Mollie-O*."

" I wish so too," said Danny. " You'd like everyone on board. Mollie's just like your own mother, Old Beaver tries to be gruff but he's nothing but a gentle soul, and Emalie and Tad are fun." Then he added loyally, " But none will take the place of you, Rob."

" I know," said Rob slowly, "and maybe after you've made a few trips upriver, you'll be allowed to take me with you."

Danny smiled, pleased.

" I'll try hard to do that," he promised.

Rob looked down at the wooden cart.

" I'd like to see what you've got," he said.

Danny jumped down from the wall.

" Come on and I'll show you."

Neither Danny nor Rob were aware of British soldiers coming out of the tavern. As Danny rummaged around in the cart, one clapped him on the shoulder.

" What do we have here? " he asked roughly. "A young merchant or a thief? "

Danny's eyes blazed.

" I'm not a thief! " he protested.

The soldier's eyes roved over the cart while a group of his companions joined him.

" You'd better make sure, Tom," one of them said.

Angry, Danny stood his ground.

" You can't touch this," he made a great mistake in saying. " This is bought and paid for and it belongs to the *Mollie-O*."

" The *Mollie-O!* " cried another soldier. " That's a hussy of a market boat that sails up and down the Hudson! " He too stepped forward, seizing Danny by the shoulders. " This makes it worse! How do we know that he's not smuggling things aboard for that petticoat of a captain? What's a woman mean, setting herself up as a captain of a ship even if it is a beat-up old packet sloop? "

Poor young Rob was thoroughly frightened but he dared to interfere.

" The *Mollie-O*'s been on the river for years," he ejaculated, " and it's not beat-up — not yet! "

Another soldier took Rob in charge.

" So the *Mollie-O*'s an old-time Yankee! " he bellowed, then he turned to his companion. " Well," he added, " I don't trust these young scoundrels! We had better board the *Mollie-O* and find out if smuggling's part of its business."

Danny was terrified now. What had he done? He had not even started being a river boy — couldn't even push a cart aboard — without making serious trouble for Mollie! His knees grew weak, and he felt like cry-

ing, but all he could do was clench his fists and walk
between two redcoats who were prodding him to push
the cart with the butt of their muskets.

Rob was being brought along too, and curious people were following in little groups.

" Old Beaver! Old Beaver! " Danny cried out involuntarily.

No answer came. Again he felt the end of a musket
poked between his shoulder blades.

" Quiet! " ordered the redcoat.

In misery such as he had never dreamed of, Danny
pushed the cart down to the water front. He had heard
what these redcoats were capable of doing. Here in
New York Town — the first port of call on the Hudson River — he was making trouble for Mollie. Danny
felt humiliation such as he had never imagined could
exist.

Would they put him on a prison ship and treat him
as they treated captured soldiers? Would Rob be made
to share his fate? And worst of all, he wondered, what
would they do to Mollie?

7

In the Name of the King!

" In the name of the King! "
The redcoats used these words like swords to pierce the brain of Danny. Once they had reached the *Mollie-O's* gangplank, they paused at the foot of it.

" Gentlemen, aboard! In the name of His Majesty, the King! "

Danny pushed the cart up the gangplank onto the deck. Scarcely had he reached the top when he saw Emalie. One look at his red-coated companions and she turned and fled like one possessed. Danny saw her disappear down the steep companionway and hoped that she was warning Mollie.

Emalie was. Almost before the soldiers could group themselves on deck, Mollie was hastening up from the companionway to join them. To Danny's utter surprise she did not fly at them like an angry mother hen as he had fully thought she might. Once she was on deck, she crossed it very slowly and spoke almost with ceremony.

" Gentlemen? " she inquired in her softest Irish voice, looking very charming. She was still wearing the flowered dress with the lace fichu which she had put on to go shopping ashore.

One of the soldiers had the good grace to be cour-
teous.

"Captain John Heath, of His Majesty's first regiment," he informed her.

Mollie's smile was compelling.

"Top o' the mornin' to you, sir," she said softly. "I
am Captain Mollie." She looked away from him a moment to the tortured face of Danny, pale as a white
rabbit's. "This is my boy," she added, "an' what is
it you are doin' to him?"

The young captain cleared his throat.

"We caught him with this cart on the street. He
says it is filled with supplies for your boat, but if there's
smuggling going on here — "

Mollie raised her hands in horror.

"Smugglin'!" she repeated. "Why, sir! Push the
cart to me, Danny, and I'll be glad to show these gentlemen what there is inside. Smugglin' indeed!" she
scorned.

Captain Heath stepped between her and Danny.

"We would rather look for ourselves, ma'am," he
objected.

Again Mollie smiled.

"You should be commended for doin' your duty as
you see it, Captain," she said. Then she turned and
looked at Danny. "But even though you're doing it,
sir, you should not be frightenin' a poor innocent
boy."

Another soldier stepped forward to join Captain
Heath but he muttered:

" Don't let a Yankee skipper tell you how to do your duty, sir."

To Danny's surprise Captain Heath answered: " Learn how to button your lip, boy, when you speak to a lady! " Facing the group of soldiers, he added, " Turn this cart upside down! "

Danny saw Mollie keep a steady eye on the soldiers as they all pounced on the cart. One by one they unwrapped the parcels and threw their contents on the deck. Small things like hardware and oarlocks they let fall and roll where they would, but when it came to rope and sailcloth, they tangled the rope into intricate knots and let the sailcloth unwind from its roll until it lay in a canvas heap clumsily billowing on the deck.

Danny had visions of Old Beaver. Apparently, he decided, the old man was still ashore. If he were aboard, Danny realized, he would have stormed and stomped and shouted and routed these redcoats from the boat even though it meant he would be taken prisoner and put the *Mollie-O* in deadly peril. Why Mollie was being as creamy as a yellow rose, Danny could not fathom. Then suddenly he knew! She was taking a cue from that Mrs. Murray she had mentioned only this morning at breakfast. The fashionable Mrs. Murray who had so charmed the British General Howe that she had made him dally around until General Putnam could escape from the trap Howe had set for him. Mollie was being smart, thought Danny. Very smart indeed! He hoped Old Beaver would stay ashore until this crisis was over.

Danny stole a glance at Rob, who was still standing

taut watching the soldiers spill the last of the supplies
out of the wooden cart. A compass was thrown down
on the deck, and there was the sound of breaking glass.
Even Mollie protested that.

" Sure now," she said to the soldiers, " there's no
need to break things."

" Quiet! " the guilty soldier growled, while Captain
Heath added, " There's nothing more than supplies
here, men, but just to be sure we'll search the ship."

" Search the ship! " Mollie repeated involuntarily,
looking down at the shambles on deck.

" In the name of the King! " said Captain Heath.

" You can be tellin' the King for me, sir, that the
Mollie-O is no smuggler! "

But Captain Heath only shrugged.

" I shall have to make sure of that, ma'am."

Mollie sighed audibly.

" Well, then, I'll be goin' along with you as a good
captain should and takin' Danny with me."

To Danny's further surprise, Captain Heath made
no objection but he motioned his men to follow him.
And never would Danny have surmised that it would
be such a thorough search! Down the companionway
they marched and into the various cabins. First it was
the galley where William was breaking eggs into a
bowl. Seeing the soldiers, he paused in the act and
looked at them with hostile eyes. For a fleeting moment Danny was sure he was going to throw an egg in
the face of one of the men who arrogantly tipped the
bowl and its contents onto the floor, but Mollie put
her fingers against her lips and murmured, " Careful,

William, these men are British soldiers! "

" As if I didn't know," growled William.

Once out of the galley they searched the cabins. First the one that Danny shared with Tad, then Old Beaver's next to it. Still Mollie made no further protest. It seemed to Danny that she was holding her tongue until they came to the cabin she shared with Emalie.

" An' must you go in there now? " she asked Captain Heath softly.

" Must," he repeated briefly.

" It's my own private place," she added in a mournful voice.

Danny stood holding his breath again, sick and trembling. Suppose — just suppose that Mollie was actually hiding something for which she could be charged with treason? It would all be his fault because he had mentioned the *Mollie-O* when he had first been questioned by these snoopy British! What would they do if this were true?

A moment of suspenseful waiting, then Captain Heath himself opened the cabin door. Suddenly he reeled and turned back to Mollie, utterly amazed.

" But — but ma'am! " he said blankly.

And even the soldiers, who had been so cocksure and jeering ever since they had come aboard, stood suddenly silent in surprise at what was greeting them now.

Even Danny couldn't quite believe his eyes. There was the usual variety of feminine things — flowered bonnets and dresses with panniers hanging in orderly rows on pegs, Emalie's sailor's shirts and pants — but dominating all else in the cabin was a picture in color showing a life-sized portrait of George III, His Majesty the King of England! There he stood against his throne, wearing royal robes of silk and ermine and a golden crown upon his head!

His Majesty the King here in Mollie's cabin! In spite of his recent fear, Danny's heart seemed to sink. Had he been mistaken? he wondered. Was the *Mollie-O* a Tory ship? Was she herself a Tory — a sympathizer of the King's as many native New Yorkers were? Was she a Tory instead of a patriot?

" Gentlemen, halt! " Captain Heath exclaimed, then he turned to Mollie. " I don't understand," he said slowly with questioning eyes.

Again Mollie smiled her rose-in-bloom smile.

" All of us encounter what we don't be understandin' these days," she said mysteriously.

Gracefully she held out her hand. Captain Heath took it and bowed low above it, holding it warmly in his own. After a moment he turned to his men.

" March! " he ordered.

Up they marched to the *Mollie-O*'s deck, Danny and Mollie following. The captain surveyed the hodgepodge his men had made of the contents of the cart with rueful eyes.

" If I had only known! " he said apologetically to Mollie.

She nodded graciously, saying, " It's often true that we must find things out for ourselves."

Again to Danny's surprise, she led them to the forward deck. He almost rubbed his eyes in unbelief

when he saw a small table already laid with a snowy white cloth and a pewter tray. A pewter pitcher, with pewter mugs beside it, stood on the tray.

Mollie took the pitcher and poured fruit punch from it into the mugs. Then she picked up the tray and gave it to Danny.

"Pass this to the men," she said, "while I serve Captain Heath."

Danny, inwardly steeped in gloom, moved toward

the British privates. To think that he was serving these men like a lackey after they had made a shambles of the cargo of the *Mollie-O!* What could Mollie be thinking of — if she were actually not a Tory? Meanwhile, the soldiers crowded around him, now in a gay and jovial mood.

"Looks very good, boy," one said, reaching out to pick up a mug brimful of a strawberry-colored liquid with slices of lemon floating on its surface.

Danny noticed the soldier's hand. It was browned by the sun and ornamented with a curious-looking ring on one finger. The ring was gold, and where one expected to see a stone or gem, this ring was hammered into the shape of a lion's head and had two sparkling green emeralds for eyes. Danny had never seen such a ring. Where had it come from?

He scanned the redcoat's face. He was as young as most of the other soldiers, fair-haired and bronzed, and his eyes were blue. Tasting the drink, he smiled down at Danny.

"Umm! Good!" he said, and drained the mug.

Again Danny caught the flash of fire from the emeralds that were the lion's green eyes. So fascinated was he by the ring, he was slow in serving the next soldier.

"What about me?" the soldier teased. "Don't I rate a drink of punch?"

None of you rate it! Danny wanted to cry out loud, but he remained silent and served the others.

Captain Heath turned away from Mollie and took a few steps toward the chattering group.

" We must be on the move now," he said, then suddenly he laid his hand on Danny's shoulder. " You're a lucky lad," he added, " to be aboard the *Mollie-O*."

Mollie conducted them to the gangplank while Danny sought out Rob, who was still standing alone where the soldiers had left him.

" What happened? " he asked Danny wonderingly.

" Plenty," said Danny gloomily.

" Are they taking over the *Mollie-O?* " anxious Rob asked.

" Almost wish they were," said Danny.

Meanwhile Emalie came darting up from the companionway and joined them.

" Are they gone? " she asked in a high whisper.

" They're going now," answered Danny.

She breathed an audible sigh of relief.

" That was a close one," she bantered. " I almost didn't make it."

" Make what? " asked Danny.

Suddenly she looked like a mischievous little monkey.

" Do you think Mollie likes those soldiers? " she questioned him incredulously.

" So it seems," Danny answered.

Emalie looked at him with disdain.

" Mollie's only acting! As soon as she saw them coming aboard I rushed down to the cabin and warned her and she told me to scatter and do my usual job! "

" What is your usual job? " asked Danny.

Emalie looked very proud.

" She trusts me to hide Jinx in the cupboard so he won't swear at the soldiers — but most of all she trusts me to hang that picture of ugly King George over the one of General Washington! "

Danny was flabbergasted.

" General Washington! " he repeated, agog.

Emalie nodded with vigor.

" Sure! It's Mollie's way of masquerading the *Mollie-O* as a Tory ship when we're in occupied waters. If she didn't," Emalie explained, " we just couldn't be patriots."

" Wonderful! " breathed Danny.

" She's a good actress," Emalie said importantly.

" A wonderful actress," breathed Danny again, then turning to Rob, he asked, " Wouldn't you say so too? "

" Well, I guess I would! " said Rob fervently.

Meanwhile Mollie approached them and Emalie said under her breath, " Now watch out for fireworks! "

They were not disappointed. Mollie looked down at the shambles on deck.

" So that's young Captain Heath," she mocked with fury. " It's a good thing Old Beaver wasn't here to see the likes of this. But when he comes back," she raved on, " he'll want to take a shotgun ashore! "

Emalie put in a word. " We'd better start upriver."

Mollie answered woefully: " Sure an' we'd better start upriver. If those soldiers come back and find out we're foolin', they'll send us all with the *Mollie-O* to the bottom of the harbor! "

8

Return of the Redcoat

Mollie was surveying the deck.

"Sure an' we'll have to get busy," she said, "an' start cleanin' up this mess. I don't know how much we can save, but we'll do the best we can. Emalie and I will start an' call William up to help us." She paused and summoned Danny to her side. "You'll have to go ashore again and find Tad and Old Beaver. Tell them to be makin' haste — it's sailin' we must do — and fast!"

Danny's eyes were questioning.

"Where is a likely place to look for them?" he asked.

Mollie thought for a moment before she answered.

"Could be like lookin' for a needle in a haystack," she sighed, "but I gave him a list of things I ordered before we sailed to visit darlin' Captain Johnny. There now, let's see. He was to pick up merchandise at the Queen's Silk Shop, at old John the Coppersmith's, and at the Coffeehouse on the Bowery. The rest of the cargo's been delivered and stored in the cargo room, and it's thankin' the good Lord I am that that pip-squeak Captain Heath didn't go and pry into it." Suddenly she smiled. " Guess he wasn't smart enough to figure a cargo room would be right up on deck as plain as the nose on his face! "

" I'm thankful for that too," said Danny.

Mollie questioned him anxiously.

" Can you remember those three places — the Queen's Silk Shop, old John the Coppersmith's, and the Coffeehouse on the Bowery? "

" That's easy," answered Danny.

Suddenly she sighed again.

" If he's not to be found at any of those, take a peek into Jason's sail shop on the water front."

" I'll find him," said Danny, then suddenly he hesitated and stood very still.

" Sure an' what's ailin' you, Danny? " she asked.

His eyes and his voice were earnest.

" This is all my fault," he said. " If I hadn't told those soldiers the things were for the *Mollie-O* — "

Mollie laid a kindly hand on his shoulder.

" Now, don't you be blamin' yourself, boy," she said. " It's not the first time we've been searched and it won't be the last." A sudden gleam came into her eyes. " As long as I've got that mug of King George to hang over General Washington's picture — may the good Lord bless him — we won't be worryin' too much. An' when we get out of these occupied waters, we won't be worryin' at all." She ran her fingers through Danny's bright hair and ordered: " Now along with you, lad. Go find Old Beaver."

He turned and nodded to Rob, who all this time had been waiting as quiet and as solemn as an owl.

" Come along, Rob," he called. " I'm going ashore."

Mollie looked at Rob too.

" So it's a friend of Danny's you are," she said pleasantly. " It's a sorry time for your visit, boy, but when we're back in port again, you may come aboard and have a spot of tea with us."

Rob's face was aglow.

" I'll be dreaming of that, Captain Mollie," he said.

" Go along with you now," she smiled as she hurried them both down the gangplank.

Rob had gracious words for Mollie.

" She's a great lady," he told Danny.

" A very great lady," Danny agreed, then thinking a long time, he added, " When she gets to know us better maybe she'll let you take a trip upriver with us."

" Oh! " breathed Rob, too overwhelmed at the prospect to be able to say more.

" Want to help me look for Old Beaver? " Danny asked as they trudged along the water front.

" You know I do," answered Rob, " and we'd better make time."

An hour later, they were disconsolate. They had been to the Queen's Silk Shop, where they found only women customers; they had seen old John the Coppersmith, who told them Old Beaver had been there and gone; and when they went to the Coffeehouse only redcoats seemed to be there, drinking China tea flavored with English rum.

" This is a good place to stay away from," Danny told Rob.

And Rob answered, " I don't want any part of it."

Suddenly they heard a boy whistling behind them. Danny wheeled around to face him.

" Tad! " he exclaimed joyously. " Where have you been? Where's Old Beaver? "

Tad grinned his slow friendly grin.

" I'm here — right here — " he began, but Danny interrupted.

" We've got to get Old Beaver quick! The *Mollie-O's* been searched by redcoats and we've got to sail! "

Tad immediately stirred to quick action for him. " You'd better follow me fast! "

He led them along through the crowded street a bit farther north on the Bowery. Suddenly he darted into the doorway of a shop above which hung a sign painted with a violin.

" But this is a music shop," Danny protested.

Tad nodded.

" Sure it's a music shop," he said. " Old Beaver's buying a new fiddle."

" A — a fiddle! " said Danny, bewildered. " But Mollie didn't say — "

Again Tad grinned.

" How could she know what Old Beaver's up to? Even her leprechauns wouldn't know that! "

Before Tad opened the door to the shop, he said with pride: " I forgot that you didn't know, but Old Beaver's one of the best fiddlers on the river. Wait till you hear him play."

Danny, still bewildered, murmured, " This is the last place I would have looked." Then he turned to Rob. " To think of Old Beaver playing a fiddle! "

Once inside the shop, they readily spied Old Beaver with a violin under his chin. He had flipped his white beard back over his shoulder, and his red shirt showed like a sign of danger. To the shopkeeper's consternation, he was running the bow over the strings, beginning to play "Yankee Doodle," the stirring song of the patriots.

"Hey!" roared the shopkeeper. "Don't play that in here! This town's full of redcoats!"

Brandishing his bow in mid-air like a sword, Old Beaver grumbled: "What do you want me to play, you yellow-livered landsman? Do you think I should be makin' music out of their 'God Save the King'?"

Meanwhile Danny rushed up to him.

"Please, Old Beaver, come with me! The redcoats have searched the *Mollie-O* and Mollie says we should be sailing. I've been looking for you for an hour!"

Old Beaver's voice had a mighty roar.

"So they've searched us again, have they, Danny?" Suddenly he delved into the pockets of his sailor's pants and brought forth a handful of shillings. "Here's the price of your fiddle," he told the astonished shopkeeper, then he turned back to the boys. "Run, boys, run!" he ordered. "We'll be hoistin' our sails before you can wink!"

But even Old Beaver could not hoist the sails quite that quickly. He had to stop at a shop on the water front to pick up another cart filled with merchandise for Mollie, then he had to make sure that the cargo he had ordered had been delivered to the boat. So almost another hour went by before Danny said farewell to

Rob, and he and Tad and Old Beaver got aboard the
Mollie-O.

Mollie was waiting impatiently.

" Sure now," she said, with her hands on her hips,
" an' why are you draggin' your heels, I'm askin',
when to dally around this town could very well be the
death of us? "

Old Beaver cocked his head on one side and spoke
with indignation.

" So I'm draggin' my heels, am I? Now listen to me,
fair Mollie. I came as soon as the boys let me know that
we'd been searched again even if I was so busy buyin'
a new fiddle."

Mollie smiled reluctantly.

" Go 'long with you now," she ordered, " and get to

hoistin' the sails. 'Tis glad I am you got a new fiddle
to play for us these nice spring evenings."

Old Beaver fingered his beard and grunted as he
turned away.

"It's an old an' mellow fiddle with strings that all
but talk." He turned to Danny as he walked on.
"You'd better come with me, boy."

But Mollie interrupted.

"I'll be needin' Danny now and Tad and Emalie
too. We've got to work in the cargo room before the
redcoats spy us sailin' out of the harbor with all these
things on deck."

Old Beaver grunted.

"Guess I can hoist the sails myself after all these
years at the helm."

Danny and Tad were about to follow Mollie toward the cargo room on deck when suddenly up from the cabin below there came a piercing cry: " Out! Out! Out! I tell you! "

" It's Jinx," cried Mollie, almost simultaneously. " Emalie put him in the cupboard when the redcoats came and forgot to let him out. Go down and tend to him, Tad."

" Thieves and robbers! " indignant Jinx was crying again.

Danny laughed out loud.

" He's mad," he said. " Good and mad."

Mollie laughed too.

" He probably fell asleep after Emalie locked him in. If he hadn't been asleep, he would have yelled before."

Danny followed Mollie across the deck to the little shanty aft. It was really only a shanty because it was constructed of secondhand boards, but strong enough to withstand the weather and protect the cargo so precious to Mollie's livelihood.

The door to the cargo room was open. Once inside, Danny stood still with surprise. Such a hodgepodge of things he had never seen gathered all together — this could very well be a general store!

In spite of the number of things and their variety, space was allotted very well. Catalogued in separate places were bonnets and shawls, slippers and colored parasols. On built-in shelves lay bolts of silk and satin, lace and challis and velvet. On other shelves were similar bolts of cotton and printed calico. Smaller items were spilled into open chests — silver buckles for slippers, the patches Old Beaver had argued about, but which were very fashionable on a lady's face. Here and there were pomanders too, in which so-called belles might carry their own perfume.

Apart from these things of vanity, there were others on the domestic side. Pots and kettles and crockery and kegs of sugar and salt. There were seeds for spring planting, balls of string, and various kinds of tea. Pairs of scissors sparkled, papers of needles and pins lay arranged in neat rows beside candle molds and candle snuffers. But what intrigued Danny most, perhaps, were the crystal jars of candy. Licorice and orange drops. Coconut, chocolate, and peppermints!

Mollie noticed his blissful look.

" 'Tis alikin' this cargo room you be, Danny? " she asked very gaily.

He nodded almost solemnly.

" It even smells good," he began, and Mollie laughed out loud.

" Sure 'an it's a sweet tooth you have." She took a candy jar down from the shelf. " Here, help yourself to the kind you like! "

Emalie was up on a ladder, putting pairs of rubber boots on a shelf.

" I'll have some candy too! " she called.

A quarter of an hour later Danny was up on a ladder too, hanging pots and kettles on iron hooks suspended from the ceiling in the rear of the cargo room. He and Emalie were working side by side when suddenly Mollie said: " It's a long time Beaver's takin' to be hoistin' the sails. We should be movin' by now. I'd better go see if there's trouble brewin'."

Leaving the cargo room door ajar, Mollie crossed the deck.

" She's right," said Emalie anxiously. " Old Beaver never takes this long to get the mainsail up."

Danny turned and looked outside.

" Look! " he cried urgently. " Old Beaver's out there too, and he's shaking his fist at someone! "

Emalie jumped down off the ladder and rushed out onto the deck. Eagerly Danny followed her.

What he saw when he reached the ship's rail made him want to cheer Old Beaver. The irate old man was still shaking his fist and bellowing down at a British soldier who stood on the cobbled quay at the foot of the *Mollie-O*'s gangplank.

" Don't you come aboard! " Old Beaver was crying. " Don't dare! We've had enough inspection for one day! " He motioned to Tad who was standing at the head of the gangplank. " Up with it, Tad! " he bellowed again. " Up with the gangplank in his face! "

Tad raised the gangplank with a jerk and the red-coat had to jump aside lest it knock him over.

" You'll settle for this, old man! " he called, outraged. " Just wait and see! "

But Old Beaver shook his fist again and turned triumphantly to Mollie.

" Guess that's showin' him," he said, vastly pleased.

But Mollie looked anxious. " I hope we get away with it," she said slowly.

Old Beaver chuckled. " We're sailin' now and they can't stop us! "

Quickly he strode away toward the helm.

Danny looked down at the soldier again. He was still standing there, glowering, when Danny had a feeling he had seen this man before. There was something familiar about him — the way he stood on his feet — a movement of his hand.

But the *Mollie-O* was already sailing. Looking again at the soldier, Danny suddenly remembered. He was sure now — absolutely sure — that this young redcoat was one of the group that had searched the boat under Captain Heath's orders. The fair-haired one with the blue eyes and the ring with the head of a lion on his finger!

Why had the redcoat come back to the *Mollie-O?* Danny asked himself, worried.

9

Trees That Go to Sea

As Danny followed Old Beaver across the deck to the helm, he repeated these questions over and over. Why had this soldier come back to the *Mollie-O* alone? And why had he wanted to come aboard? Could it be, Danny wondered, that Mollie's little ruse had not been successful after all? Had Captain Heath only pretended to believe that Mollie was a Tory, in spite of the picture of the King hung so prominently in her own private cabin?

Danny found himself bleak with sudden fear that Mollie had outsmarted herself. Perhaps this redcoat with the curious ring had been sent back to spy upon the *Mollie-O* before it could sail out of these waters which were under the domination of the British flag. The fact that Old Beaver had prevented the soldier from coming aboard would be another serious mark of misconduct against the *Mollie-O*.

It is good, thought Danny now, that I was asked to pass that fruit punch. If I hadn't noticed that soldier's ring, I wouldn't have picked him out of the group and wouldn't have remembered what he looked like.

Still thinking hard as he took his place beside Old Beaver, Danny decided to keep his own counsel. He wouldn't tell anyone, not even Mollie, about the suspicion he now felt, but if the soldier turned up again! Even then he doubted whether it would be wise to frighten Mollie until he was sure his fears were well grounded.

" Watch now, Danny," Old Beaver's voice brought him back to the business at hand. " Watch me take my *Mollie-O* out of this British harbor! "

He watched the old river man skillfully maneuver the boat out of its berth until it started sailing with the wind. They had actually been berthed a bit to the west side of Manhattan Island, so it seemed as easy tack to veer the *Mollie-O* onto its course up the Hudson River.

As Old Beaver sailed expertly between a frigate and a freighter, Danny spoke admiringly: " That was very close, sir. How do you manage to do it? "

Old Beaver answered: " The secret of good sailing, Danny, is to keep your sails full of wind. If you don't remember that, your boat will drift to leeward or she'll refuse to sail just as a stubborn mule balks at walkin'."

Danny, wanting to remember this, repeated: " Keep your sails full. Keep your sails full of wind."

And so it was full sailing now up the broad, majestic river. Soon the church steeples of New York Town with their glittering golden spires and the houses with their weather vanes seemed to grow smaller.

On either side of the river were low-lying hills with

forests clad in the green of springtime. Willows, here and there, dipped graceful branches over the edge of the Hudson shore, freshening their leaves in the sky-blue waters. White birches glistened in the early May sunlight. Stalwart old oaks and maples flaunted new and shining leaves while here and there a dogwood tree lighted the whole tanglewood with flowers so white they glittered like stars.

Against masses of rhododendron with its showy pink and purple flowers were the somber evergreens. These were the ancient ones of the forest, standing on guard like grandfather trees. Hemlock and spruce spread their branches above the river while the proud white pine trees stood tall and straight and strong like the valiant mariners that they really were.

Danny looked at these forests with interest. Trees and winds and waters had always seemed to speak to him. If he had not had " salt water in his veins," as his mother had sometimes said, he would have wanted to become a woodsman. He had heard about the famous Daniel Boone, who had blazed the trail through the wilderness of Kentucky and was even now commanding a company of soldiers to repel savage Indian attacks in this war against the British.

Thinking of these things, Danny was saying, " The Hudson shores are beautiful."

Old Beaver nodded and answered: " They're God's own, I'm thinkin', Danny. Guess I have some backwoodsman in me." He pointed to a group of trees growing close to the water's edge. " See those tall trees over yonder? Do you know what they are? "

Danny stared at the evergreens.

"They're pine, I know, but I don't know what kind."

Old Beaver glanced at them with affection.

"They're white pine in the woodsman's book, but I have a special feelin' for them because I know they're seagoing trees."

"Seagoing trees?" repeated Danny incredulously.

"Yes-sir-ee," said Old Beaver, "those white pine trees go to sea!"

"But — but — " Danny began.

Old Beaver was warming to his subject.

"See how straight and tall their trunks are?" As Danny nodded, he went on, "Well, those trunks are used for masts — you can't get anything better. If a mast of a ship is made of good American white pine, the ship can sail the seven seas and buck all kinds of stormy weather." Old Beaver leaned on the tiller as he went on with enthusiasm. "Why, the King thinks they're his own royal trees. Up until this war began they were reserved for the Crown."

"Reserved for the Crown!" repeated Danny, now really impressed.

Old Beaver nodded vigorously.

"As far back as 1691 a charter was granted by William and Mary to the province of Massachusetts, reserving for their so-called Majesties all white-pine trees with a diameter of at least two feet. They even put their brand upon them — what was called 'the King's broad arrow' — and took in the other colonies' growth of trees until white pines became the chief articles of

American exportation." Old Beaver turned the tiller while his eyes gleamed. " Yessir-ee, boy, we've got the old King's dander up because we won't export them now. Many a British ship is going right to the bottom of the sea because they can't get white-pine trees to build masts with! "

Danny looked back over his shoulder to the clump of evergreens disappearing beyond a turn in the river.

" Do we have many of these trees, sir? " he asked Old Beaver.

" Many! " exclaimed the pilot. " Why, we've got hundreds of thousands of acres — not so many down here — but up above the Tappan Zee they cover whole mountainsides. They're sturdy trees too, grow ninety to a hundred feet high — some even two hundred — and they live to be three hundred fifty, sometimes four hundred years old! "

Danny quickened with surprise. It seemed such a wonderful thing — this tree that went to sea. To think of its growing two hundred feet high and living to be four hundred years old!

Suddenly he looked up at the mast of the *Mollie-O*.

" Is the *Mollie-O*'s mast of white pine? " he asked.

Old Beaver beamed with pride.

" It's as straight and gallant a mast as you'll find — and it came from the white-pine forests up beyond the Catskills."

Danny was more intrigued than ever.

" It must be a loss to the British Navy if we won't sell them these trees for masts."

Old Beaver laughed aloud.

" Now you're really catchin' on. They'd cut our throats to get them. They tried to stop us from cutting them down so we couldn't have good ships to sail, and that's one of the reasons why we colonists put our backs up! " Again Old Beaver laughed. " It wasn't all a case of dumping tea into Boston harbor an' gettin' all riled up against the Stamp Act! " He bent so close to the tiller that his long white beard got in the way but he paid no attention, so stirred was he by his subject. " Well, now, it's us that won't let them cut down our white pines, and they're losin' more ships for want of good masts than even the King will admit! "

Danny smiled and rubbed his eyes.

" Good," he murmured, " good." Suddenly he blinked as the *Mollie-O* rounded a turn. " But look over there, Old Beaver! There are rocks on the Jersey shore towering up like a fortress! "

Old Beaver smiled his rakish, crooked smile.

" Could be a fortress, Danny, yes, could very well be. Those rocky walls you're lookin' at are the Palisades."

Danny kept his eyes fastened upon the rocky heights rising vertically from the shore close to the water's edge. Rugged and majestic, they glittered in the golden light of afternoon. As the *Mollie-O* veered close to the western shore, Danny was fascinated, held speechless by their beauty.

" My, but they're high! " he said.

Old Beaver nodded.

" Aye, they're high, boy. Some are over five hundred feet and they stretch out like a wall along the

river for miles and miles."

"No wonder they're called the Palisades," mused
Danny.

The old skipper agreed.

"People say they're given that name because they

look like the log palisades that protect outlying settlements, but I don't rightly know whether that's true or not. Seems likely enough. An' the rocks that form them are very old — traprock and sandstone — so they tell me, mixed in such a way that there are only a few other rocks like them in the whole world."

"The Palisades," repeated Danny. "They ought to make a good lookout."

Old Beaver smiled.

"Right you are, Danny." He pointed to a rock that jutted out beyond a turn in the river. "See that spot right up there? Well, that's where General Washington stood and watched the British take Fort Washington across the river. He was lookin' through field glasses, watchin' the redcoats outnumber his men until it must have made him sick at his stomach. Over here at Fort Lee he had only a handful of men and was powerless to do anything about it."

Danny's eyes were grim.

"That was a black day for us," he said.

"A very black day," repeated Old Beaver.

Danny watched him turn the ship into a channel, mid-river, then he looked back at the Palisades crowned with trees and foliage like the green-gold crown of a king. He was about to tell Old Beaver that he would like to walk on top of the Palisades someday, when Emalie came racing toward them in her usual spirit of flight.

"We'll soon be in port," she called to Old Beaver. "Mollie says we're putting in at Yonkers and should berth before supper."

Old Beaver grumbled as he always did at Emalie's so-called " orders."

" Oh, she did, did she? " he mocked. " Well, maybe I'm just hungry enough I won't berth the ship until I get somethin' to eat."

Lighthearted Emalie, quite without malice, seemed all concern. She went close to Old Beaver, stood on tiptoe, and whispered gaily in his ear.

" I can snitch something for you from the galley or the biscuit barrel."

" Biscuits! " roared Old Beaver. " Save them for yourself and Jinx! It's more than a biscuit I'll be havin'."

Emalie backed away and scolded, " You'd better not spoil your appetite for supper by eating now." Suddenly she winked at Danny. " And I'd like to borrow Danny if you can spare him."

" And just what for? " Old Beaver asked. " He'll never learn to be a river boy by just taggin' around after you."

" But Mollie wants him," Emalie protested.

Old Beaver kept his eyes on the helm.

" Scat, then, both of you."

" Come on, Danny, hurry! "

Emalie laughed and hurried away, and Danny had no choice but to follow.

10

Pirates in the Night

" Are you sure Mollie wants me? " Danny asked Ema-
lie suspiciously.

Emalie shook her head.

" Honest and true," she babbled. " I have to help
William in the galley, and you have to give a hand to
Tad so the cargo room is ready when people come on
board to buy things."

Danny gave a start of surprise.

" Are we going to sell things today? " he asked.

Emalie's laughter was as clear as a bell.

" Of course we're going to sell today — as long as
it's daylight. That is what the *Mollie-O* is for. We'll be
in Yonkers two whole days."

" Two days! " echoed Danny.

" We stay two days in every port," Emalie said importantly. " That's why it takes so long for us to go
upriver. If we didn't stop to sell things, we could make
it from New York Town to Albany, with good sailing
weather, that is, in twenty-four hours. Other boats do."

" I never thought of that," said Danny, " but after
all, Mollie has her living to make."

" Her living and the *Mollie-O*'s," added Emalie.

" And even ours. She gives us a shilling to spend every Saturday, or didn't you know that, Danny? "

Danny nodded vigorously, remembering how pleased he had been when Mollie had told him about what she jokingly called his " Saturday payday."

" And she wouldn't have to, either," he was telling Emalie, " when she gives us food and shelter. I never saw a shilling when I worked for Widow Reeves and I worked harder than I'm working now."

Emalie tilted her face windward and sighed.

" Someday," she said softly, " I'm going to pay Mollie back for making my living for me now."

" I am too," vowed Danny.

What kind of living Mollie made was shortly to be clear to him. Old Beaver had no sooner berthed the *Mollie-O* at the little Dutch town of Yonkers than women and girls, some singly, others in groups, swarmed aboard. Mollie stood at the top of the gangplank, welcoming each girl or matron as she came onto the boat. There were many whom she called by name.

" How do you do, Mrs. Moore? It's a charmin' thing to see you, ma'am." Then to a young matron wearing a blue challis dress and a pink Cashmere shawl, " Hello, Elizabeth, how are you? " Then to a round-faced Dutch housewife who carried an empty market basket, " How do you do, Frau Schaegel? " and to a rosy-cheeked little Dutch girl with flowers on her bonnet, " It's very pretty you are lookin', Gretchen."

On it went, and she greeted many, almost twenty, Danny counted. He and Tad were stationed in the cargo room ready to show any men who came aboard the boots and garden tools and seeds.

Mollie ushered the women into the cargo room to show them what she had brought. Danny noticed she was being very careful to give them the feeling that they were more than welcome to look, even if they did not buy. And how they looked made Danny gasp with amazement.

" These Dutch housewives can't be fooled," Tad whispered to him, grinning. " If I were Mollie, I'd tell them to scat unless I saw they meant to buy."

" But Mollie's smart," Danny whispered. " She makes it slow and easy for them to decide."

But how women handled things! mused Danny. He would have liked to slap their fingers. One picked up a bolt of silk and draped it around herself like a bright-red cardinal's cassock dragging on the floor. Another unwound what looked to Danny like yards and yards of lace, pinning it, meanwhile, to a half-finished jacket that she had brought to get the exact effect. Still another matron took the glass lids off the spice jars and sniffed cinnamon and pepper until they made her sneeze!

" That pepper should have blinded her," Tad laughed unfeelingly.

It seemed that this was ladies' night to shop aboard the *Mollie-O,* because no men appeared for Danny to wait on. They were still standing guard when Mollie prepared to close the cargo room for the night.

" Sellin's over, boys," she told them cheerfully. " Come on out on deck. Old Beaver's going to try out his new fiddle."

Danny and Tad followed her eagerly. Stars were shining above the river, and there was the soft sing-song of waters lapping against the sides of the boat. Old Beaver was already sitting in his favorite deck chair, his fiddle tucked under his chin. He played Irish songs for Mollie, and many other ballads. When Old Beaver played his fiddle of an evening, even the river seemed to listen.

So entertaining was he that even Emalie listened quietly until he swung into a lively dance tune which she recognized as a country jig. She jumped up like a dancing doll.

" Dance with me, Danny," she urged. " Come now, dance with me! "

He looked at her, grinning, but inside he felt shy! Emalie looked very pretty tonight. Mollie always made her dress up for selling. She was wearing a flowered skirt with a pink bodice, although she had no taste for it.

" I said, ' Dance with me, Danny,' " she repeated, going toward him.

" Get up on your feet, boy," smiled Mollie.

" Glad it isn't me she wants to dance with," Tad snickered.

Danny looked embarrassed as he found himself getting up on his feet, but when he went whirling across the deck with Emalie he found it could be fun.

" Good, Danny! " she cried. " Someday you'll be a wonderful dancer! "

" Someday! " he replied scornfully, and twirled her

around in a really difficult dance step just to show he knew how.

The moon was riding high when Mollie shooed them all to bed, all except Old Beaver, who had laid down his fiddle and picked up his Dutch meerschaum pipe which he always smoked as a " nightcap."

Suddenly from Yonkers there came the voice of the Town Crier:

" Ten o'clock and all is well! Ten o'clock and all is well! "

Climbing into his bunk above the one where Tad already lay dead to the world, Danny had a haunting thought. He was suddenly wondering if all was as well as it seemed. Even during the fun on deck he had thought again of that soldier, the one with the lion's-head ring, who had come back to the *Mollie-O*. A lion was a strong and dangerous creature. Had the sight of its emerald eyes in the ring on that redcoat's finger been a bad omen?

Danny was not superstitious, but in these days of spies and bitter counterspies one couldn't be too careful. He must keep his eyes open lest this soldier turn up again as he had threatened Old Beaver he would. And if he did? Well, Danny vowed in this moment, he would protect the *Mollie-O* with all his heart and all his strength.

After breakfast the next morning, Danny stood on the deck of the *Mollie-O* watching the sunshine dappling the river. The little town of Yonkers looked as peaceful as though far away from the drums of war.

People were riding on horseback or in carriages. Many were walking in and out of shops, doing their morning marketing. Busy Dutch housewives, wearing little white caps and aprons, carried market baskets. Danny saw one full of live chickens. Somehow the pleasant scene made his thoughts of the soldier with the lion's-head ring seem like an ugly dream.

He was still looking over the town when he felt a hand on his shoulder. Old Beaver stood behind him. He was carrying a bundle of rope.

" Well, boy," he said in his usual grumbling way, " it's time to stop dawdlin' an' get to work."

" Yes, sir," said Danny.

Old Beaver's eyes sparkled.

" With all your yen to sail a boat," he challenged, " I'll wager you don't even know how to tie a sailor's knot. Or do you, Danny? "

Danny grinned infectiously.

" Not yet, sir," he confessed.

" What did I tell you? " Old Beaver mocked. " Well, since we'll be in port all day, it's a good time to begin. Ever hear of a knot called Englishman's tie? "

" Never," said Danny.

" It's a good strong knot for joining ropes," Old Beaver told him, " an' there's another called a cat's paw, which is a good knot to tackle, but we'll begin with the easy ones. Pay attention now and we'll start tyin'."

In the next few hours Danny learned that there were enough knots in a boatman's life to make him dizzy. First, there was the single or overhand knot that formed the basis for all others. There were sheet bends for joining ropes, sheepshanks for shortening rope, granny knots for slips and jams, stevedore's knots to prevent unreeving. And there were scores of others, which Old Beaver didn't even mention at their first knot-tying session.

Meanwhile, Mollie, Emalie, and Tad were taking care of customers who came aboard the *Mollie-O*. Over Old Beaver's shoulder, Danny could see them come and go. One pretty girl was going off with a bolt of calico. A big Dutch housewife was carrying a copper kettle. A boy in Dutch pantaloons carried a pair of boots in one hand and a pewter pitcher in the other. Danny could hear Mollie say to him: " It's careful you must be of the pitcher, Hans. Don't be lettin' it get scratched."

Presently Old Beaver stood up.

" Guess you'll be learnin' how to tie 'em, Danny. You're doin' pretty good. Only the sheepshank you haven't got the knack of, so keep tryin' while I go ashore an' see if I can learn how things are going up along the Tappan Zee. We'll be berthin' there tomorrow night."

Berthing on the Tappan Zee! Danny found himself excited at the prospect. He had heard a lot about that body of water rolling wide and deep in the shadow of High Tor, a legendary mountain. Under the very noses of respectable sloops and frigates of war, pirates were known to hide out there, big and burly river pirates. It was said they gloried in the fearful storms that swept down from the mountain as though brewed by witches. Of all the places on the Hudson River, so it was said, the waters of the Tappen Zee were most frequently illuminated by lightning, which traced its crazy course overhead, trailing zigzag streaks of silvery flame. Yes, thought Danny now, it would be a wonderful thing to berth in the Tappen Zee!

But not until evening when he and Mollie and Emalie and Tad gathered on deck to see the rising of the moon did he learn more about it. Old Beaver was in a mood to tell stories. While he smoked his pipe, he looked out on the river and began to talk.

" Aye, I've a feelin' for High Tor, who lords it over the Tappan Zee. An' sure as you're born I've seen the ghosts that people say be up there! "

" Ghosts! " repeated Danny, thrilled.

Old Beaver leaned forward, his narrow slits of eyes alight.

" From the top of High Tor, Danny, it's a quarter of a mile straight down to the Tappan Zee. And you can see fifteen miles or more of river north and south. The choppy waters roll along with the salty ocean tides, and it's a great sight to behold."

Emalie, who was sitting cross-legged on the deck in front of Old Beaver, interrupted.

" Get to the ghosts, Old Beaver."

" Is it no patience you're havin', Emalie? " Mollie scolded meanwhile.

Old Beaver frowned.

" Mind your manners, Miss Flibbertigibbet, an' I'll get to the ghosts without your help! " Then he looked at Danny. " They say when Henry Hudson sailed his

Half Moon on the Tappan Zee, he lost one of his ships. The crew climbed up High Tor, they tell me, to keep a lookout for a ship to help them, but none ever came. Some say the Indians got the crew and scalped them."

" Oooh! " shivered Emalie and Tad.

Old Beaver went on.

" Anyhow, on dark nights before the storms that blow so wild up there people say you can see the ghosts of the crew walkin' around wailing like banshees."

" I'd like to see them," said Danny, impressed.

It was Mollie's turn to shiver.

"If you ever saw a banshee or ever heard it wail," she said, " you'd never want to see another, even on the Tappan Zee."

Moonlight flooded that body of water when the *Mollie-O* arrived there twenty-four hours later. Old Beaver brought her to anchor under the frowning cliffs of High Tor. There were other ships anchored there too. One was a slave ship with a white captain. One had a deck piled high with logs that it was carting down from the Hudson Highlands. And one was a mystery ship, for it flew no flag.

" Pirates! River pirates! "

The words went from ship to ship like a high alarm, but it was also understood by unwritten law that if these river pirates created no hostile action or made no attack, they too would be left in peace.

The children hoped to catch a glimpse of the pirates in person, but strangely enough all evening, while Old Beaver sat spinning yarns, not one came onto the deck

of the pirate ship. Where were they hiding? Danny
wondered. Old Beaver ventured the opinion that they
were probably not on the ship at all but off somewhere
on shore, peddling ill-gotten loot.

It was only when Danny and Tad were getting ready
to go to bed that the strange thing happened. Tad was
already stretched out on his bunk when Danny said:
" I noticed a very bright star not far away from the
moon tonight. It was shining right over Old Beaver's
shoulder. I think I'll look at it through my spyglass."

" It's cold up there now," protested Tad, " and everyone on board's asleep."

" I won't make any noise," promised Danny.

He picked up his spyglass, which he kept in the corner of the cabin, and went up on deck.

He raised the glass to his eye and fixed it on the
brilliant star. He never knew how long he had looked
at it — perhaps five minutes, maybe ten. He had almost decided that the star was Venus when suddenly
he heard the sound of voices on the narrow trail that
skirted the nearby Hudson shore. Were these the
voices of pirates returning to their ship? he wondered.

Slowly he lowered the spyglass to bring the wooded
trail in focus. Silvered by moonlight, it was almost as
bright as it would be by day. Then he saw them coming —

" Pirates! " he gasped excitedly. " Real river pirates! "

They were wearing red bandannas, and their dark
hair straggled down their backs. Danny could see them
as plainly as if he were walking along beside them.

Suddenly he gasped again. Many of these men were toting iron-banded chests — but not all of them were pirates. Two of them were soldiers!

Feeling a tingling sensation along his spine, Danny lowered the glass a bit to bring the soldiers into focus. Were they, like the pirates, renegades too, perhaps deserters from the Army? With a wave of sudden shame he saw that both were wearing Continental uniforms. They were actually American soldiers then, but what could they be doing here on the Tappan Zee in such disreputable company?

Again and again, Danny maneuvered his spyglass. Finally he brought it into a position where it was fixed

on the faces of the soldiers and he could make out their features. As though he had been struck a sudden violent blow, Danny wheeled backward.

He had seen these men before. One was Captain Heath who had headed the search of the *Mollie-O* and the other was the redcoat who wore the lion's-head ring on his finger!

11

"Not Long for the River"

Excited, Danny kept holding the spyglass up to his eyes. Keeping it fixed on the now oddly familiar figures, he tried to get it into position so that he might see the soldiers' faces again. He didn't want to risk being mistaken. He wanted to be sure that he recognized the men.

Danny looked long and hard. He was right — just as he had thought. And what were these British soldiers doing here — disguised as American soldiers and consorting in the dead of night with pirates on the Tappan Zee? This was a hard question to answer, yet Danny felt he must try because he had the ominous feeling that whatever they were doing was linked with the fate of the *Mollie-O*. If this were not true, he pondered, why had the soldier wearing the ring returned to the boat in New York Town? And why had he threatened Old Beaver who had prevented his coming aboard?

The mystery deepened as Danny kept watching the exciting scene on shore. The pirates carried their chests aboard their own ship, but the soldiers stayed on the trail. Once the chests had been put down on deck, Captain Heath gave the private a definite order. Danny saw the young man turn and walk away into the woods. Meanwhile, the captain talked with the pirates. Danny wished he could hear what they were saying, but since he couldn't, he could only wait to see what would happen next.

Presently he saw. The private was coming back from the glade leading two horses already saddled. He brought one to Captain Heath who mounted it without delay, then he himself mounted the other. Giving a parting salute to the pirate ship, the captain called two single words and this time Danny heard.

" Hannah's Rock," said the redcoat distinctly.

The captain of the pirate ship repeated: " Aye! Hannah's Rock, sir."

Then before they cantered away, the private turned his horse so that it was facing the quiet *Mollie-O*. At a touch of his whip, the animal reared high on its hind legs. The soldier shook a threatening fist at the *Mollie-O* just as he had done on that day when Old Beaver had directed Tad to lift the gangplank to keep him from coming aboard.

In another moment, both turned their horses northward and were riding on the moonlit trail that zigzagged along the shore of the Tappan Zee.

Danny took his spyglass down from his eyes. Then he stepped out of the shadow from which he had been watching. What had he seen? he wondered. He shivered, not so much with cold as with excitement. What had he really seen? Was all this a part of a plot the

British were hatching with these pirates? It had to be British, he knew, because these soldiers were British, even though they were disguised now in American uniforms. They had to be disguised, he was thinking, because they were in American territory, just as the *Mollie-O* had been in the British occupied zone when she had been in New York Town.

Danny's teeth began to chatter. Surely he had started all this! When Old Beaver had trusted him to take the cart back to the boat he, Danny Beckwith, had started all this trouble. He, alone, was responsible now. Why, he questioned himself in vain, had he been such a ninny as to tell those redcoats the cart belonged to the *Mollie-O?* But they would have found out, he realized bleakly. Somehow they would have found out.

Again he looked at the pirate ship. The pirates were carting the chests below. It looked as if there were a dozen men, or maybe more, now that they were all assembled. What was in those chests? Danny wondered. And did the captain's final words mean that they were to be delivered to a place called Hannah's Rock?

Still another question occurred to him. Why were these soldiers traveling on horseback instead of on a boat? If they were really concerned about those chests, why hadn't they taken passage with the pirates to go to Hannah's Rock themselves? And what part could the *Mollie-O* play in all this?

Danny felt suddenly weary. He had better go to bed, he thought, and get up with the sunrise to see what he could aboard the pirate ship. He felt there would be no more action there until dawn because the pirates had gone below. They too would probably sleep — and then —

But there was little sleep for Danny. He tossed around in the upper bunk until he woke up Tad in the one below.

" Hey, Danny, up there! " called Tad. " You're rolling around like a whale in the ocean."

" Sorry," said Danny, " go back to sleep," and he tried to settle down.

Perhaps, he thought, still wide-awake, he should let Tad in on this growing mystery. Tad and Emalie too. Perhaps if they worked as a team, they could come nearer to solving these questions. Why were these soldiers traveling on horseback? What was contained in those pirate chests, and if they were going to Hannah's Rock, where was Hannah's Rock? All these questions had to be answered and most important of all, Were they planning revenge against the *Mollie-O?*

Still tossing on his bunk, Danny decided to tell Emalie and Tad what he had seen. He and they too must stand guard over Mollie.

So he lay thinking hard until sunrise. It dawned very bright on the Tappan Zee. Long before anyone was up, Danny hastened up on the deck to see if the pirate ship was still there. He was just in time, it seemed. The river pirates were setting the mainsail preparing to sail on the broad stretch of water.

Danny could hear them talking as he leaned over the *Mollie-O*'s rail.

" Aye," one big dark-haired fellow was saying, " we'll head upriver while we've got a spankin' breeze." Suddenly he looked toward the *Mollie-O,* and seeing Danny, grinned. " What's the matter with the lady? " he called. " Don't her skipper know enough to heave-ho with the wind? "

Danny couldn't help smiling a friendly smile. To think he had heard a pirate — a real live pirate — talk to him! And what would the pirate have said if he knew that Danny had seen their goings on in the dead of night?

Still looking at the pirate, Danny saw him make a mock bow and call out again.

" We're off now, boy," said the pirate. " Pieces of eight to you now and gold and silver in your pocket! "

" Thank you, sir," called Danny, intrigued, then added, " we'll be following you upstream! "

Suddenly the pirate threw back his shaggy head and roared: " That's what you think, boy, but I know better! The *Mollie-O*'s not long for the river! "

Danny stiffened.

" The *Mollie-O*'s not long for the river! "

The words rang in his ears like a warning bell as the pirate sloop took to the wind and sailed away.

Danny's heart was beating fast as his thoughts whirled on and on. So he had been right in thinking there were plans already laid for the *Mollie-O*'s destruction! How much time did he have to prevent it — and how could he prevent it if he did have the time? Neither he nor Emalie nor Tad could carry out any plans they might make until they could get more information. And how they could come by more, confined as they were on shipboard, he could not fathom.

He felt himself smartly slapped on the back. He whirled around to see Old Beaver standing behind him.

" Mornin', Danny," he said, enjoying the boy's surprise. " You be up early, ain't you? "

Danny pointed toward the white sails of the pirate sloop rounding a blue bend upriver.

" I was awake with the sunrise," he answered, " and when I came on deck that pirate ship was hoisting sail."

" Good riddance," muttered Old Beaver. " An honest skipper never knows what those ruffians will do."

Danny looked grim.

" Right you are," he told Old Beaver, " but one of them even spoke to me."

Old Beaver was all ears.

" What'd he say, Danny? "

" You really want to know? "

" Why else would I be askin'? " Old Beaver growled.

Danny put on a slight show to hide the gnawing fear inside him.

" Well," he drawled, " he wanted to know what was wrong with the lady, meaning the *Mollie-O*."

" There's nothin' wrong with her, did you tell him? She's as gallant a one as ever put her shoes down deep in the Hudson River! "

" But that wasn't all," laughed Danny.

" Well, what else did the robber say? "

" Well," drawled Danny again, very slowly. " He wanted to know if the *Mollie-O*'s skipper didn't know enough to heave-ho with the wind? "

Fiery Old Beaver stomped his feet.

" Oh, he did, did he? " he exploded as Danny saw
Mollie coming up behind him. " I know more about
this river than they can tell you about the seven seas!
I'll hoist the sails," he went on irately, " and I'll run
all over 'em long before we round Bear Mountain! "

Mollie laughed aloud.

" Go on with you," she said. " It's away ahead of
yourself you are! We'll be puttin' in at Haverstraw before we round Bear Mountain. I've got to get rid of our
cargo before we go chasin' pirates! "

Old Beaver shook his fist in the direction of the pirate sloop's fast disappearing sails.

" I'd like to cut their ears off," he roared.

Mollie laid her hand on his shoulder.

" Down to the galley with you, Old Beaver. It's high
time you're havin' breakfast." Turning to Danny, she
called, " It's poison a pirate sloop is to him."

Once at breakfast the atmosphere cleared. Old Beaver became even jovial as he always did when his be-
loved Hudson waters were the subject of the conversa-
tion.

" Like to hunt? " he asked Danny.

" Wouldn't object to shooting a partridge or even a
bear," Danny grinned.

Old Beaver sniffed a steaming cup of coffee.

" When we get up to Bear Mountain," he drawled,
" you may have the chance."

Emalie spoke up knowingly.

" But the woods up there are full of people as well
as wild life now. Redcoats and our own men are hiding

out waiting for action."

Old Beaver nodded.

" Aye," he went on, " I heard that too. The good townspeople of Yonkers say there'll be plenty of patriots workin' up on Constitution Island, buildin' new defenses. Last year there was action there after Washington's defeat at White Plains, and General Clinton knows full well there'll be action there again this year."

" I hear that General Schuyler," said Mollie, " has brought five hundred men down from Albany to help build a blockade. Sure an' they'll have to have their defenses ready when the redcoats strike again."

They're not the only ones, thought Danny. We've got to start building defenses of our own to protect the *Mollie-O*.

But Emalie was squirming in her chair. Old Beaver watched her, silent for a moment, then he bantered: " What's wrong with you, Little Miss Flibbertigibbet? You're squirmin' around like a fishin' worm! "

Emalie laughed out loud.

" Guess I am," she replied, " because Tad and I would like to go fishing and take Danny with us. Don't you know the shad are running? "

Mollie looked indulgent.

" So they are," she said slowly, " and this is a good time for all of you to fish. We can't be sellin' cargo here on the Tappan Zee. Get your fishin' lines while you have the chance." She looked at Danny inquiringly. " Want to go, boy? "

Danny got up from his chair with eagerness.

" Well, I guess I would," he answered, but then he looked at Old Beaver. " Unless, sir," he added, " you may need me."

Old Beaver smiled his crooked smile.

" Away with you, lad," he said, " you're only young once."

A little later all three sat on the riverbank, fishing poles in hand, but all three, too, had lost interest in fishing, even for the silvery shad that played in these Hudson waters. Danny was holding the others spell-bound with his story of what he had seen in the night.

" Pirate chests," breathed Emalie, " just think of it, Tad. Real pirate chests! "

" Wonder what's in them? " Tad asked, both surprised and baffled.

Danny spoke soberly.

" That's what we have to find out," he said, " but most of all we've got to stand on guard to learn why the pirates said that the *Mollie-O*'s not long for the river."

Tad and Emalie sat upright, simultaneously shocked.

" Not long for the river! " they repeated, aghast.

Danny nodded.

" That's what the pirate said when I told him we'd be following them upstream. He just stood there laughing and called: ' That's what you think, boy, but I know better! The *Mollie-O*'s not long for the river! ' "

Emalie's bright eyes darkened.

" It's those soldiers," she said slowly. " They're good
and mad at Old Beaver and Mollie, so they're planning
to destroy us. And somehow those pirates will help
them."

" Smart girl," said Tad. " I think you're right."

Danny stood up in the tall grass.

" Guess we'd better sign in blood," he told them.

" Sign in blood! " Emalie almost squeaked.

Tad sat upright too.

" I know what he means," he told her. " Danny
thinks we should band together and sign in blood to
protect the *Mollie-O*."

Emalie was not quite convinced.

" Couldn't we just band together and swear to protect her without the blood? " she asked squeamishly.

Danny shook his head.

" It's your blood or nothing," he announced, " but
if you're afraid, Emalie — "

" Afraid! " she cried scornfully. " I'm not afraid of
anything! "

" We'd better do it now, then," said Danny, moving
solemnly away from them toward a silver birch tree.

" What are you going to do? " Emalie asked.

" I'm going to peel off some birchbark," he answered, " then we'll take our oaths and sign our names
in blood on it." Plucking a thorn from a nearby bush,
he added, " We'll use this to write with."

Tad and Emalie stood by. Very, very soberly Danny
smoothed out the birchbark he had peeled from the
tree until it was as smooth as a piece of onionskin.
Then he turned to the others and spoke seriously.

" Repeat after me," he announced. " I, Emalie," he began.

" I, Emalie," she repeated.

" Do solemnly swear," Danny went on, " to help Danny and Tad protect the *Mollie-O* — "

" Do solemnly swear to help Danny and Tad protect the *Mollie-O* — " she repeated, and her eyes widened as Danny continued, " with my hands, my heart, and my very life."

" With my hands, my heart, and my very life."

After she had repeated his words, Danny gave her a long black thorn.

" Prick your finger with this," he said, " and sign your name on this piece of birchbark."

Emalie was not quite so dignified when it came to pricking her finger.

" Ouch! " she exclaimed as she dug in with the thorn and squeezed out a drop of blood.

" Sign here," said Danny, holding out the birchbark.

Emalie signed, then sighed: " There! If that doesn't make me a full-blooded member, I don't know what does! "

The ritual was repeated for Tad, then Danny himself took the solemn oath, but when he had finished he looked long at the *Mollie-O*. His eyes were bright with affection as he gazed steadily on the ship's white sails. " I only know," he went on slowly, " that Mollie and the *Mollie-O* are the dearest things on earth to me and I'll really guard them with my life."

" Amen," said Emalie, not meaning to be funny.

Even Tad did not laugh at her fervor.

" I'll say, ' Amen,' to that too," he said rather hoarsely.

On the deck they saw Old Beaver striding toward the helm. Meanwhile Danny wheeled around to face them and asked suddenly, " Where's Hannah's Rock? "

Both looked absolutely blank.

" I never heard of it," said Tad.

" Neither have I," said Emalie.

Danny looked troubled.

" The soldiers mentioned it to the pirates — as their next meeting place, I think."

" Must be a secret name for somewhere," Emalie pondered.

Danny nodded his head.

" That's what I think too," he said, " but we have to find it."

12

The Tory Gunsmith

Hannah's Rock . . . Yes, they all decided, it was a name to reckon with. Surely it must be along the river, but where? There were all kinds of rocks — big and little, high and low — along these Hudson shores. And what did the soldiers mean to do when the pirate chests were delivered there? Most important of all, how could all this carry out the threat that the *Mollie-O* was not long for the river?

Danny was asking himself these questions as he stood at the helm beside Old Beaver. The ship had taken off from its berth in the shadow of High Tor, and was riding the choppy waters out of the Tappan Zee.

" What's our next stop? " asked Danny.

Old Beaver didn't take his eyes from the river.

" Haverstraw, Danny," he answered.

" What's at Haverstraw? " asked Danny.

Old Beaver smiled and shook his beard.

" Well, for one thing," he drawled, " there's an old cobbler who always fixes Mollie's shoes. Otherwise it's a town on General Washington's route to West Point, an old town, Danny, settled by the Dutch. Some of them raise flax and wheat on its outskirts, others are merchants, and still others hunt and trade with the Indians for skins. They're good solid people and many are our customers."

" Seems the whole Hudson valley's Dutch," laughed Danny.

" Most of it but not all," replied Old Beaver. " Remember, even Mollie's the daughter of an Irishman who came here from Galway and settled south of Black Head Mountain. But now," he added, " you had better scuttle down to her cabin and see if she's got any shoes to be mended. We'll be in Haverstraw in a few minutes."

Danny hastened down to Mollie's cabin where he found her sitting at a table, going over what she called her " cargo books." In these she kept account of what she bought and sold on each of her trips up and down the river. Danny appeared in the doorway, and she looked up and smiled.

" Well, Danny," she asked, " what's on your mind now? "

" Shoes," said Danny, smiling too. " Old Beaver says we'll soon be in Haverstraw and he wants to know if you have any to be mended."

Mollie rose from her chair.

" Sure an' he knows I have," she said. " There's one of Tad's and a pair of mine and two old slippers of Emalie's. How that girl wears out her shoes so fast, I'll never fathom, but she's always got holes in them." Mollie took a bag down from a peg in the wall. " Here's a whole bagful, Danny, an' when we get to Haverstraw you may take them to Han's place."

" Hans? " repeated Danny.

Suddenly Mollie laughed.

" He's a little old cobbler in a little old house. He sits at his cobbler's bench an' hammers away on the soles of old shoes as if his life depended on it, which I suppose it does; He has three sons helpin' to fight this terrible war, an' one o' them's an aid to my darlin' Captain Johnny."

" I will like seeing Hans," said Danny. Then, as Mollie gave him the bag of shoes to be mended, his eyes sought the portrait of General Washington hanging on her cabin wall for everyone to see.

She noticed his questioning look.

" And what is it now, Danny? "

He hesitated a moment before he answered with a worried look in his eye.

" It's that picture, Mollie. I'm always afraid someone will see it who shouldn't, and it will cause you trouble."

Mollie tousled his hair with affection.

" Now don't you be worryin', Danny. Patriots all up and down the river love this picture of our general, an' when the redcoats come along, as you know, up goes the picture of their King! "

" Yes," nodded Danny, " but — "

" But what? "

Again Danny hesitated before he said, " Maybe you won't always get the King's up in time."

" Speakin' of spies? " she asked him point-blank.

" I guess I am," he confessed.

Mollie put her hand under Danny's chin until his face was tilted so that she could look deep into his eyes.

" That's a chance we have to take," she said in her low, rich voice. " We all have to take it in days of war. But the most important thing, Danny, is to know how to be prepared to meet trouble when it comes."

" Guess you're right," he agreed soberly.

But actually he left her cabin feeling at sixes and sevens, as Emalie would have put it. Mollie felt she was right — and yet — well, she hadn't seen the goings on in the dead of night. She didn't know that Captain Heath and his friend with the lion's-head ring were now disguised as American soldiers and had met with river pirates on the Tappan Zee. Nor did she know about the chests loaded on the pirate ship to be delivered to a mysterious place called Hannah's Rock. Worst of all, she did not know that a pirate had told him that the *Mollie-O* was not long for the river.

For a moment Danny was tempted to reveal these dangerous happenings. But he realized that, if he did, Mollie would have nothing to strike back at yet. The soldiers were in the saddle, riding the narrow trails on the Hudson shore. The pirate ship had already sailed to the north ahead of them. And Hannah's Rock was a place of mystery that had as yet to be discovered. No, decided Danny, Mollie should not be frightened by all these ominous things until he could find out how and where to combat them. He and Emalie and Tad must do this for her without fail. Somehow they must keep their vows already signed in blood.

Danny sighed audibly. Being a river boy seemed to

comprise so much more than learning to sail a ship!
And that too was harder to learn than he had ever imagined. Old Beaver had been right when he had said
it would take a long time. And yet, as Danny emerged
from the narrow companionway and strode across the
deck toward the cargo room, he let his gaze rest on the
flowing river as though it were a silver chain to be captured and worn around his neck.

" Danny! Danny! " Old Beaver called from his place
at the helm.

Danny turned away from the cargo room where he
had meant to join Tad.

" Coming, Old Beaver," he answered.

Once he had reached him, Old Beaver instructed,
" Stay here and pay 'tention now, Danny, while I
swing into Haverstraw."

Danny looked at the little port with its cobbled
streets and gabled houses, then along the shore upriver
where he saw a misty mountain rising high above the
waters.

" Is that Bear Mountain yonder? " he asked Old
Beaver.

The old skipper nodded.

" Sure is," he answered, " and it is one of the reasons
why the Hudson is called the great river of the mountains. After we leave Haverstraw, we'll be entering the
Hudson Highlands, and there you'll see wild country,
boy, and what Mollie calls grandeur."

" I'll like that," said Danny.

Old Beaver kept his eyes on the river, veering out of
the path of a frigate, threading his way among a num-

ber of sloops already at anchor in Haverstraw waters.

"Pay 'tention now, Danny," he said again, "an'
watch how I lower the mainsail a little. The wind is
getting stronger an' I have to make a slight turn."

Danny watched closely as Old Beaver lowered the
mainsail and set the jib before he swung a bit leeward.
Meanwhile he ordered Danny: "Throw the anchor
overboard now. This spot needs no sounding."

Danny hastened to throw the anchor. Then he said,
"If you do not need me now, sir, I'll take Mollie's bag
of shoes to the cobbler."

"Run along, Danny," Old Beaver agreed.

Picking up the shoe bag he had thrown down on the
deck when Old Beaver had called him, Danny hastened off the ship. He wished he could have taken Tad
with him but he realized that Tad would have to re-
main aboard to help Mollie in the cargo room.

Once on the main street of Haverstraw, Danny
looked for the sign of a painted shoe hanging over a
shop. That must be Hans's place, he thought, as he
saw a swinging boot just ahead, and I'd better get rid
of these shoes before I look around the town.

The Dutch cobbler sat at his bench — he was a little
old man and very busy. He wore dark pantaloons, a
cobbler's apron, and a brightly embroidered waist-
coat. He had a fringe of gray hair around his bald head
and sat sewing on shoes, hunched up like a gnome.
Danny watched him for a moment before he said,
"Good morning, Hans."

The cobbler looked up with the bluest of eyes.

"Good morning, boy," he replied and smiled.

Danny walked across the shop to him.

" Mollie of the *Mollie-O* has sent me here with these shoes," he said.

To his great surprise, the little old cobbler dropped his awl, rose from his bench, and held out his hands.

" Vonderful, vonderful Mollie," he cried. " Velcome to you, boy! Velcome! Come in and share a pitcher of milk."

" Thank you, sir," said Danny, pleased.

Hans took the shoes Danny had brought and put them on his bench. Then he walked to a shelf on the wall and took down a big blue pitcher. There were two matching cups on the shelf and in a moment he was filling them with foaming milk.

" Milk is goot for growing boys, ya? " he was saying.

So it was they began to talk. Danny told Hans all about himself, and Hans, in turn, told Danny about his own boyhood in Holland, the land of windmills and tulips and dykes.

Hans started working again as he talked. His cobbler's bench faced the window on the street side of his shop, so he could see all that happened outside when he glanced up from his work. Danny was facing the window too. Suddenly he laughed, amused.

" Ya? " questioned Hans, not looking up. " You see something funny? "

Danny pointed to a long-legged man in a shopkeeper's apron chasing a pig down the street. It was giving him a merry race and squealing all the while.

" Look, Hans," laughed Danny, " that man and the pig— "

To his sudden surprise, Hans's round face darkened and his eyes filled with scorn.

" Pigs is goot for pigs," he said. " That man is Richard Winston, the gunsmith, who has the shop next door. He's one of the blackest Tories in the whole Hudson valley! "

" A — a Tory! " Danny exclaimed. " You mean he's on the side of the redcoats? "

" Ya, what else? " asked Hans. " I have nothing to do with him! And one day soon he'll be brought to justice! " " So will other Tories," Danny almost said aloud, thinking of those who had said that the *Mollie-O* was not long for the river.

The gunsmith was coming back up the street, the runaway pig in his arms.

" The pig's name is Gertrude," Hans enlightened him. " Others keep dogs, but he keeps a pig for a pet."

Danny noticed, then, that the rosy little pig was wearing a blue ribbon. Suddenly he had an exciting thought. This man, Richard Winston, was a Tory and would be in sympathy with those British soldiers. Perhaps he would know of Hannah's Rock!

13

Voice of the Storm King

A few moments later, Danny left the cobbler's shop.
Hans must not know, he had decided, that he planned
to visit the gunsmith. Once out on the street, he
walked back toward the *Mollie-O,* then retracing his
steps, he made a wide circle around the cobbler's shop,
and approached the gunsmith's from a side street in
the rear.

The shop was dark and musty inside. All kinds of
muskets and rifles stood in stacks against the wall or lay
side by side on the merchant's counter. Danny could
hear him talking to Gertrude, the pig.

" I'll put you in a pen," he was threatening, " where
you'll have to live like other pigs if you keep running
away."

The pig was standing near the counter, looking up
at him comically. Danny had never realized before
what a pet a pig could make! Its flesh was clean and almost pink, its eyes were china blue, and its funny little
tail curled around and around like a pretzel!

" I beg your pardon, sir," Danny attracted the gunsmith's attention respectfully.

The man looked up with surprise.

" I didn't see you come in, boy," he said. " What is it I can do for you? "

" I'm a chore boy on the *Mollie-O,*" Danny said boldly, " and I'd like to buy a cartridge box for Old Beaver."

At the mention of the *Mollie-O,* Richard Winston's eyes looked dark and piercing. Suddenly he snapped: " I don't sell cartridge boxes to boys," he said sharply. " Old Beaver should know that. Tell him to come for one himself."

Still Danny spoke respectfully.

" As you like, sir. I will." Suddenly he turned and half smiled. " But perhaps you'll be good enough to give me a few directions. I want to go to Hannah's Rock."

" Hannah's Rock! " the gunsmith bellowed. If Danny had told him he wanted to go to China or exotic Tibet, the man could not have sounded more highly disturbed. Danny pretended not to notice.

" It should be near here, shouldn't it? " he asked politely.

Richard Winston looked white with rage. With a snarl and savage gesture, he reached across the counter to lay his hands on Danny and hold him fast. But Danny dodged quickly and raced toward the door.

" Come back here! " shouted the gunsmith. " Come back here — or I'll — I'll — "

Danny was already headed for the street. By the time Richard Winston had dashed out from behind his counter, Danny was running as fast as his legs could

carry him back toward the *Mollie-O*. He never stopped
until he reached the gangplank even though his heart
was pumping so fast he feared it would leap right out
of his mouth!

Richard Winston hadn't followed. He didn't dare
follow, thought Danny triumphantly. He couldn't take
a boy prisoner out in broad daylight! People were
coming and going along the main street of Haverstraw.
Someone would be sure to interfere with a man who
tried to capture a boy — and the man a well-known
Tory at that! But now I know, thought Danny, in glee,
there *is* a Hannah's Rock somewhere and it must be a
Tory stronghold!

Emalie and Tad were coming out of the cargo room
as Danny walked up the gangplank.

" Hey! " he called across the deck.

They came toward him, running.

" You're all out of breath! " Emalie cried, startled.

" Guess I am," laughed Danny, " and I'll tell you
why."

They went into a huddle close against the rail.
Danny told them about his meeting with the gunsmith
and how he had dared to ask directions to Hannah's
Rock.

" How could you be so brave? " Emalie asked in
great admiration.

" It's a good thing he couldn't reach you across that
counter," said Tad. " He might have ordered you
shot! "

Danny looked undisturbed.

" I'm not worrying about being shot," he said. " I'm

only glad I know that Hannah's Rock exists and only Tories know about it."

"It must be upriver," Tad was musing. "We can't have passed it yet or we would have seen the river pirates' ship anchored near the shore."

"You're right, Tad," said Emalie, while Danny added: "From now on, we stand guard. One of us must stay on deck with my spyglass fixed on the shore. We'll take turns and watch for anything that looks like a pirate ship or a rock or even a soldier on horseback!"

"Good," said Emalie, pleased. "I'll start right now."

"But suppose it looks suspicious," said Tad, "and Mollie or Old Beaver — "

Danny interrupted. "Tell them we're playing a game," he advised. "A secret game all our own." After a pause, he asked, "What's the next port?"

"Bear Mountain," Tad answered.

So each of them took turns standing guard. Faithfully they kept watch, changing every daylight hour. Seeing one or the other standing at the prow of the boat, holding the spyglass fixed on shore, Mollie did become curious.

"Sure an' what are you lookin' for?" she asked, amused.

When Danny told her they were playing a secret game all their own, she only nodded indulgently, and Old Beaver grunted something about "queer young-'uns."

Before they reached Bear Mountain, he herded them all together on deck. Here, he told them, was the en-

trance to the Hudson Highlands and he didn't want
Danny to miss the splendor of the panorama. Looking
northward, Danny saw mountain peak after mountain
peak towering above the swiftly flowing river.

Old Beaver said: " There's Dunderberg, the Thunder Mountain, over on the western shore, and to the
east you see the granite ledges of Anthonys Nose.
These two mountains be the ones that form the gate-
way to the Highlands, and it's a sayin' of the Dutch
that by the light that plays around them you can always gauge the weather."

Danny saw the rugged peaks royally clothed in blue
and purple.

"Does that bluish light," he asked, "mean the
weather's to be fair? "

Old Beaver nodded.

" Sure does," he answered, " but if the Storm King's
set to walk along the Storm King Trail there, the
mountains lose their heads in mist the color of silvery
smoke. Then all the river boats have to beware. The
Storm King makes his thunder roll louder than a
witch's curse, and his lightning strikes the river in
tongues of flamin' fire. I've seen as many as fifty sloops
hidin' out here near Bear Mountain, waitin' for the
crazy wind to blow itself out."

Danny pointed to lofty, rock-covered peaks rising in
grandeur behind Dunderberg Mountain.

" Are those the Shawangunks? " he asked.

Again Old Beaver nodded.

" They're real Injun peaks," he answered. " The
River Tribes have powwows there, the like you've

never seen." He turned back to Danny. "Watch me veer the sails now, boy, while we put in at that wooden pier under Bear Mountain. Hunters and trappers are waitin' there for Mollie to bring them hunting knives and shootin' gear."

Danny watched attentively. When the *Mollie-O* dropped anchor at the well-worn wooden pier, the men were waiting, as Old Beaver had said.

They were a colorful lot in their fringed hunting shirts and coats and coonskin caps with tails hanging down. They carried muzzle-loading rifles slung over their shoulders. Some dangled game they had shot in this wilderness — bright-winged partridges and pheasants, rabbits and raccoons, a beautiful spotted fawn.

Suddenly Danny gave an excited little cry.

"There's an old man with a bear, and the bear's alive!"

Old Beaver grinned.

"What do you think Bear Mountain's named for? There are rocks up there so full of caves that baby bear cubs tumble all over the place." He smiled as he looked toward the old man holding a half-grown bear by a rope attached to a leather collar. "That's Sim Smith an' his dancin' bear waiting for me to play the fiddle."

"Oh," breathed Danny. "Oh, good!"

When the *Mollie-O* had berthed, the hunters swarmed aboard.

"Mollie, Mollie!" they called out affectionately, meanwhile slapping Old Beaver on the back. "Aye, I see you've made it again!"

Mollie appeared in the doorway of the cargo room.

" Sure an' I've got powder horns," she called, " and your huntin' knives too! "

Emalie, followed by William and Tad, raced up from the companionway. Emalie was carrying Old Beaver's fiddle.

" Here's your fiddle," she was calling. " Is Sim Smith here with Black Bruin? "

As Emalie gave Old Beaver the fiddle, Sim and his black bear came aboard. Danny saw with delight that the bear had been brushed until his fur shone. His eyes had a droll and friendly look, and he acted as though he fully expected to be asked to dance and show off.

" Black Bruin's a clown," Emalie told Danny. " He dances for us every time we stop here. And, of course, he's always paid."

" Paid? " echoed Danny.

" In sugar," laughed Emalie. " He eats it right out of my hand."

Old Beaver began to tune up his fiddle. Suddenly he lifted his bow. He swung into a dance tune, and at the sound of the first note Sim let Black Bruin free. The bear got up on his hind feet and began to dance. Some of the woodsmen clapped their hands in time to the music, others kept tapping their feet until Black Bruin, delighted at all the attention, whirled and twirled like a Spanish dancer.

" Here, Bruin, here! " cried Mollie, and obediently he danced toward her.

She was wearing a bright-red apron, which she took off and put on the bear, and so pleased did he seem

with the color that he kept bowing and bowing like a performer after a show.

" He's wonderful, just wonderful! " cried Danny.

" He lives with Sim in a cabin up there on Bear Mountain. Sim says he's as smart as a coon dog and understands everything Sim says," Emalie told Danny.

Old Beaver kept on fiddling. The dance went on until the bear was weary enough to stop his clowning and beg for sugar from Emalie. Meanwhile the men followed Mollie into the cargo room. They bought the hunting knives and powder horns she had brought from Manhattan, and some bought boots. And, as always, when they gathered on the *Mollie-O*, Mollie made an occasion of it and offered them refreshment. They talked about the war and the rumors they had heard of the new defenses the Americans were building up here in the Highlands.

Danny was listening to these rumors when suddenly the men seemed in a hurry to go ashore. He heard one of them say, " The Storm King's brewin' one of his quick ones. We'd better get started if we want to reach camp."

Danny looked at the afternoon sky. He was surprised to see that the clouds were no longer pearly with sunlight. Up over Dunderberg Mountain they were hanging dark and heavy. Down along the Storm King Trail the branches of trees were beginning to sway with a fitful wind.

" It looks so stormy all of a sudden," Danny cried.

Old Beaver heard him and nodded.

" That's how the Storm King makes 'em. Sudden

and fierce enough to take your breath away." He waved to the departing woodsmen. " Hope you make it back to camp, boys. See you next trip! "

Even Black Bruin seemed eager to head for his home on Bear Mountain. He strained at his leash, pulling Sim along.

Mollie stood in the doorway of the cargo room, watching her departing friends.

" Sure an' this will be a bad one," she said.

Almost at once the thunder started to roll from peak to mountain peak. Dunderberg, the Thunder Mountain, seemed to hurl it northward toward the Catskills, and they tossed it back again in crash after crash after crash. Lightning silvered the jagged peaks of the Hudson Highlands, outlining them with angry fire. On the narrow Storm King Trail making its way along the river, the Storm King himself seemed to be carrying lightning flashes in his hands to hurl far out on the churning waters. The river was writhing under his fiery touch.

Danny and Emalie and Tad watched the storm from the cargo room's porthole.

" They're always bad in the spring," said Tad, " but this one is a monster."

On into the evening it roared, then in a mood that seemed uncanny, the Storm King suddenly held his fire, the rain became a gentle shower, and all in a moment, ceased. Mottled clouds disappeared from the sky and the moon rose like a princess on a silvery throne.

~

Danny stood watching it from the deck an hour later. Only he was awake enough to be prowling around the ship. Mollie and the others had gone to bed early. Even Jinx, the parrot, had called: " Get to bed now! Get to bed! " but Danny hadn't listened.

He was leaning over the guard rail, looking down at the moon-shadowed waters. He could hear them lapping against the shore because the *Mollie-O* was berthed close to the Storm King Trail running parallel to the river. Suddenly he blinked his eyes, for there seemed to be little flashes of flame reflected in the waters. These did not come from the light of the moon!

He lifted his eyes from the river to the forest along the shore. Immediately his heart started pounding. The flashes were coming from torches held by wraith-like figures close to the water's edge. He picked up his spyglass, which he had beside him, and held it up to his eyes. He wanted to see by the light of the moon how many of these creatures there were — and who were they? Hunters? Trappers? Fishermen? Indians? River pirates? Soldiers?

Whether or not they saw his gesture, Danny was never to know, but by the time he had the glass in focus the figures had disappeared and all he saw was the flame of a torch being extinguished among the trees.

Danny stood for a moment, perplexed. Who were these men? he wondered. Did they have a camp there in the woods or were they here to spy upon the *Mollie-O?* He took the glass down from his eyes, suddenly knowing what he must do. He must go into those woods and see!

He seized the *Mollie-O*'s rope ladder and threw it down over the side of the boat. Flinging caution to the winds, he climbed down it hurriedly, and in only a moment was standing on the Hudson shore.

There was no light in the woodland now. No flame flickered to give him a signal as to which way to go. He stood for an instant, looking this way and that.

Suddenly terror swept down upon him. He could hear himself scream but he could see nothing now — nothing at all. Someone had sneaked up behind him and covered his head with a gunny sack. And he was being carried off — he knew not whether to land or water.

14

Hannah's Rock

*" Get him into the boat! " he heard a man's voice com-*manding.

He felt himself roughly pushed, then almost bodily lifted, into a boat. Again he was pushed hard and felt himself stumbling, this time down onto a wooden seat.

" Now take the oars," the harsh voice ordered, " and we'll get to Hannah's Rock as fast as we can make it."

Hannah's Rock, thought Danny, almost elated. Now I'll really know where it is! But why were they taking him with them? he wondered, as he heard the gentle drip-drip of water from the oars. It wasn't long before he found out.

" Take that gunny sack off your head," one of them commanded.

Danny tugged at the sack and soon he had it lifted up over his head, tousling his hair in the process. Once he laid eyes upon these men, he was not really surprised. Captain Heath of His Majesty's regiment and the soldier with the lion's-head ring!

" You two! " Danny spoke almost with scorn.

Captain Heath answered him grimly.

" Aye, Danny Beckwith," he said, "and it's going
to be harder for you than it was that day in New York
Town. You're getting too big for your britches — like
the captain of the *Mollie-O*. We know she's a patriot
instead of a good Tory — we've made it our business
to find out! " His voice became lower with wrath.
" And you thought you'd ask the gunsmith how to get
to Hannah's Rock! You made a big mistake there, boy.
Now you'll see where Hannah's Rock is and you won't
like it at all! "

Danny looked up at the Highlands where the peaks
were outlined in silver. Somehow they seemed a fabled
land on the horizon. Hannah's Rock must be up there
among them — but who was Hannah, actually? he
wondered, strangely enough for the first time. She
would have to be a Tory since she was in league with
these British brigands — but what kind of woman
would she really be?

Suddenly he shivered thinking of what the captain
had said. He vowed, however, not to show fear. No
matter what they might do to him — even if he were
so afraid his very flesh was crawling — he must never
show it.

But the private was speaking jeeringly now.

" Another thing we found out," he said, " is that
Richard Winston's to be depended on."

" Aye," laughed the captain, " even a man who
keeps a pig has no stomach for rebels."

Again he looked at Danny, who gave no sign that
he had heard. In the ominous silence that settled now
on the dugout, he remembered Old Beaver saying that

the river would talk to him of " good men and bad
from the ends of the earth."

Good men and bad, pondered Danny. Well, Old
Beaver, he was thinking, looking at Captain Heath
with his musket between his knees, I'm with the bad
men now. What they will do when they leave the river,
I have no way of telling yet — but you, Old Beaver,
please take care of Mollie!

He looked back at the *Mollie-O*'s anchor lights until
a bend of the river made them disappear from view.
Meanwhile the men rowed on and on.

" Hannah had better be ready and waiting for us.
We have no time to lose," the captain said finally.

" Aye," said the private, " no time at all," and
Danny saw the lion's head on his finger seem to take
fire from the light of the moon.

Another bend in the river and he could see a wooden
pier standing deep in Hudson waters. Mountains rising behind the landing looked like giant warriors
asleep in silvery shields, and looking up at these Danny
saw the rock!

It was big and grotesque and jutted out like a stone
terrace halfway up the mountainside. A little cabin
was built on it — a veritable cabin of the winds because it would face the brunt of them when they swept
down from the peaks or up from the river — in full
view below.

" Pull in close to the landing, Silas," the captain directed, and that was the first time that Danny had ever
heard the private's name.

" Aye, sir," answered Silas, and soon the boat was

grating on little stones scattered on a narrow beach.

Captain Heath kicked Danny hard in the shin.

" Out with you," he ordered, " and make fast tracks for that narrow trail winding up the mountain! "

Pain shot up through Danny's leg. Quick tears welled in his eyes, but he got out of the boat, as ordered, and almost hobbled along toward the mountain path.

" You go ahead, Captain," said Silas, holding his musket ready, " and I'll guard him from behind."

Captain Heath brushed Danny aside with another blow that landed in the middle of his back. The captain strode on ahead, flinging words over his shoulder.

" If he makes a move to run," he told Silas, " give him a bullet and fast! "

" Aye, sir," answered Silas, " it would be a pleasure."

So Danny walked imprisoned between them and when they started to climb the mountain he felt the butt of the musket prodding him between his shoulders.

" Don't be so slow, boy," Silas warned, " or I'll give you a bullet to make you dance right up there to Hannah's cabin! "

Danny tried to hurry even though he was cringing from the pain still throbbing in his leg. He could see Captain Heath striding on ahead. At a zigzag turn of the trail, he saw that the rock was just above them. A candle burned in the cabin window.

Suddenly he heard an almost unearthly growl.

" It's that infernal dog," Silas called to the captain. " Hannah's still got him."

Once on top of the rock, Danny saw the dog — large and powerful and crouching. He was tied to a tree near the cabin door.

" I'd like to kill that beast," said Captain Heath as the dog bared his teeth, but he stood stock-still and cried: " Ho, there, Hannah! Call off your dog! "

The candle in the window flickered as it was picked up by a woman's hand. In another moment she opened the door.

" It's all right, Prince," she said to the dog, and immediately it was quiet. " So you've come," she said briefly to Captain Heath. " I've been waitin'."

Then Danny had his first glimpse of her. She was a middle-aged woman with a sallow, yellow face and straight black hair that straggled to her shoulders. She had the features of an Indian but she was partly English.

She must live here all alone, thought Danny. No wonder that she keeps a dog.

Hannah led the way into the cabin, holding the candle high. It had only one room and a lean-to kitchen. A big black kettle hung on a crane in a huge fireplace, and on the shelf above it was a stuffed owl.

The captain spoke as he entered the room.

" Greetings, Hannah," he said briefly, " we've come right on schedule. I hope the chests did too."

Danny almost stopped breathing so eager was he for her answer. So the river pirates had already been here!

Hannah's answer was revealing.

"Aye, they've been delivered and I've already sent them on to the — " She looked at Danny suspiciously as though she feared to give concrete information. After a pause, she continued. "Well, I sent them on to their destination. There were close to a hundred guns, and good ones. Where those pirate rascals got them, I'll never be able to fathom." Suddenly she stopped again and looked point-blank at Danny. "But what about this boy?" she insisted.

Captain Heath laughed.

"We had to bring him along because he already knows too much. He's a chore boy on the *Mollie-O*," he added significantly.

Danny almost smiled. Apparently the captain had not guessed that he had shared all he knew with Emalie and Tad. The moment that they found him gone, they would tell Mollie and Old Beaver everything they knew.

"I'll make good use of him on the trail," Captain Heath said.

The trail, mused Danny. So they were taking a trail from here!

Hannah put the candle on a table, then she went toward the fireplace.

"I'll make you a cup of tea," she said, "an' then you can rest a few hours."

Captain Heath looked puzzled.

"See here, now, Hannah," he said slowly, "it's high time you talked. Day after day since we left Manhattan we've been surveying the white-pine forests. In all this

enemy territory we've found no white pines tall enough to be of any consequence — even those marked with the King's broad arrow."

As the captain talked, Danny's thoughts were spinning. So they had been traveling on horseback to inspect the forest lands where the white pines grew! They were surveyors as well as soldiers!

Danny remembered what Old Beaver had told him about these stately trees. How they were claimed by the King to be used for making the masts of sailing ships even long before this war had started. The royal charter of 1691, Old Beaver had told him, granted by William and Mary to the province of Massachusetts Bay, had reserved to Their Majesties all white-pine trees with a diameter of at least two feet! Such trees were later branded with the King's broad arrow, and similar reservations were made by Queen Anne, George I, and George II. Restrictions on pine-cutting had enraged the colonists as much as the Stamp Act or the Boston Tea Party. They had helped create the tension that had started this Revolution against the mother country.

Old Beaver had even called the trees — those wonderful white pines — the trees that go to sea!

But Captain Heath was still talking.

"You sent us the maps you made with the aid of the Indians. We've tracked down every pine forest they showed but still found no pines big enough to be cut for our largest masts. Our vessels have to be bigger than the rebels'. British ships are going unbuilt because we can't get tall pines, and since we can't — "

He paused for a moment while Hannah looked at him, repeating, " Since we can't, Captain Heath? "

He looked her straight in the eye and said: " Our only alternative, Hannah, is to set fire to the rebels' supply or they'll have enough ships to win this war! With John Paul Jones on the high seas now — "

Danny's eyes were large with shock. His heart was fluttering like a caged bird inside his breast.

Set fire to the white-pine forests to cut off the Yankee's supply!

Everything was clear now. The soldiers had ridden into the hills to survey the forests for the Crown. Tory Hannah had worked with the Indians, had tried to mark her findings on maps, but none of the trees yet found had proved to be big enough to make good masts for the British. Meanwhile the soldiers had acquired rifles from the river pirates to bribe the Indians up here. All of it, thought Danny, was strangely like a puzzle that he could now very easily fit together.

Captain Heath was growing angry.

" Look, Hannah," he almost shouted, " you must have other maps here, and we can't take time to dally. We've spent enough time now without getting good results."

Hannah looked at him sullenly.

" I'll show you the maps," she promised, " but you won't want to use them."

Captain Heath stood his ground.

" Can you give me one good reason why? "

Hannah fingered her black apron.

" Because," she went on, " the white-pine forests

north of here are dotted with Indian villages."

Captain Heath laughed aloud.

" Who cares for Indian villages? Are you such a bad
Tory you'd let the rebels keep their trees rather than
burn a few Indian huts? "

Still Hannah delayed.

" But some of these Indians have been almost
friendly toward the British. It is even thought that they
may be persuaded to help our General Burgoyne."

Captain Heath shrugged.

" Very few would help us. And the King would
gladly lose them to cut off the rebel supply of white
pine." Suddenly he went closer to Hannah and looked
down at her, demanding, " You get those maps! "

She turned her back on the captain and crossed the
room to a corner cupboard. She opened the door of it
sullenly.

" Here are the maps," she said. " You can study
them for yourself. I've got the red coats you ordered
too, so you can appear like the proper British soldiers
you are! "

" Good," said Captain Heath. " Now you may make
us that cup of tea, and after an hour's rest we'll take
the trail to the forests." Finally he turned to Danny.
" There'll be no tea for you, boy. You're going hungry
for a spell."

Silas looked at Danny too.

" And you might as well start working. This cabin's
cold. There's a woodpile at the door. Go get another
log and throw it on the fire."

" And be quick about it," added Captain Heath.

Slowly Danny crossed the room to the door. Looking back over his shoulder, he put his hand upon the latch. A cold, clean wind blew into the room as he opened the door and went out.

Once outside, he started running as though his feet had wings. He would escape from Hannah's Rock and take what he had learned to someone in high authority. He would save those forests from being burned! He would save the trees that go to sea!

But Danny had reckoned without Hannah's dog. Discovering Danny, he howled like a famished wolf on the trail of a lost lamb. The cabin door flew open and out came the soldiers in hot pursuit.

He had gone, perhaps, a hundred feet when he felt their hands upon him, dragging him down to the ground. Rolling him over and over, they started beating him hard with the butt ends of their muskets.

" We'll teach you not to run," Captain Heath said.

Before he felt his eyes close and all go black around him, Danny was conscious of Hannah coming toward them with a lantern in her hand.

15

Danny at the Helm

It must have been almost an hour later that Danny be-
came conscious enough to be aware of what was going
on around him. He was smart enough not to open his
eyes lest the captain should start tormenting him, but
vaguely he realized he was lying in front of a blazing
fire in the cabin. He could smell apple-wood logs burst-
ing into flames. Peering through half-closed eyelids he
saw the soldiers sitting at a table where Hannah was
pouring tea.

Lying completely motionless, pretending to be still
unconscious, Danny heard Captain Heath say: " You
deserve a medal, Hannah. It was a smart move to have
those chests delivered to the Tory hide-out under High
Point Mountain. From there we can have them carted
to wherever we trade with the Indians." Suddenly he
laughed heartily. " The redskins should be glad to ex-
change good solid muskets for the privilege of burning
down a few trees."

" Aye," agreed Silas, laughing too.

Hannah, however, looked grim.

" It won't be a few trees you'll be burning — it's

whole forests of good white pine."

" All the better," asserted the captain. " The sooner these rebels run out of masts for their ships, the sooner we will win this war." He got up from the table and stood looking down at Hannah sharply. " And what plans have we got for the *Mollie-O?* While we're in the forest burning down trees, who will trim the sails of that hussy? "

For a moment Hannah was silent. Captain Heath became impatient.

" Well? " he challenged her irately.

Toying with her napkin, Hannah mused a moment before she answered.

" I know that plans are being made for takin' her over but I haven't heard what kind yet. I reckon the King's agents in New York Town are not too keen about giving out too much information at one time. I have been told to expect counsel on the *Mollie-O* — but that's all I've been told."

Captain Heath looked disappointed.

" I'd like to know what they plan to do with her before we take the trail. It would warm my heart to think that she was going up in flames the same time as the trees."

The *Mollie-O* in flames! Danny felt sick inside. He had been shocked to learn about the destruction planned for all those trees that go to sea — but to think of the *Mollie-O* being burned! His head throbbed with pain at the thought, and he almost put his hand up to his eyes when he realized that, if he did, the Tories would know he was conscious and realize he had been listening. But the *Mollie-O* in such dreadful peril!

He listened again to Hannah's voice.

" You've no time to lose, believe me, Captain. You'll find the trail little more than a footpath and sometimes not even that. Indians enter the Catskills only for hunting — and I'm told that even the Sopus tribe do little lingerin' there. It is all too wild and forbidding. But you will have to cut through a portion of the mountains to get to where the white pines grow."

" Let's have another look at the map," said the captain, spreading it out on the table while Hannah moved the candle to obtain a better light. " Here's High Point Mountain," he said, putting his finger on the spot; then tracing a line on the map with his other hand, he went on. " Here's our Tory hide-out. You say we're to follow the Rondout River to Eddyville Falls to enter the Catskills by way of Stone Ridge."

" That's right," said Hannah, peering closer at the map, " and right here's Millwheel Gap, our secret hiding place for Tory ammunition. That's where you'll find the new batch of rifles to take to the Indians."

" Good," said the captain, " very good. You've saved Silas and me the trouble of trying to cart them that far."

Again Hannah looked at the map with critical eyes.

" Instructions for further transportation of the rifles will be given you at Millwheel Gap where they'll probably have Indian guides to do the carrying for you. From Millwheel you've got a long way to go — maybe even as far as the Susquehanna shore."

Silas looked over Hannah's shoulder and when he spoke his voice was grim.

"We've got a long hard trip ahead of us. I think we should start right now."

"He's right," said Hannah to Captain Heath.

The captain turned away from the table and picked up his gunny sack from the floor.

"We'd better check our supplies again," he advised, delving into his gear.

Silas picked up another sack that lay on a nearby chair.

"I'll look to my own," he said, alert.

Meanwhile Hannah folded the map that still lay on the table. While Danny watched her furtively, he saw her turn and look at the soldiers still occupied with their gunny sacks. Then he saw her do a very startling thing. Again she eyed the soldiers — then stealthily, very stealthily, she slid the map under the tablecloth and brought forth what looked like another one folded in the identical way!

Danny almost got to his feet. Was Hannah really switching the maps or was he actually seeing things? He watched her almost wide-eyed, then he saw her move toward the soldiers with the substitute map in her hand.

"Here is the map," she told the captain. "You'd better put it into your sack."

"Thank you," answered Captain Heath. "I've a special pocket here."

Slipping the map into the sack, he finally faced Hannah. "Everything's in order now," he said. Suddenly he looked at Danny. " Everything but him."

Hannah looked at Danny too.

" If you know what's good for you, Captain, you'll leave that boy with me."

The captain looked puzzled.

" But I said we could use him on the trail. He'll make a good target as well as a chore boy."

" Target? " echoed Hannah.

" Indian target," explained Captain Heath. " Who knows but we may need a decoy. We're dealing with savages."

Hannah looked down at Danny again.

" You'll be better off without him," she said. " I know Indians. I've worked with them here. I know they are prone to make captives of boys while they find great amusement in killing soldiers. And if they should take this one captive," she went on carefully, " and he should tell them what he knows, our whole Tory hide-out would be in danger."

Silas waited for the captain to speak, but when he seemed to debate an answer, Silas spoke first.

" Hannah's right. I think we should leave the boy here. It would be different if she wasn't a Tory."

Captain Heath was still reluctant.

" But I intended to punish him by making a slave of him on the trail."

Again Hannah spoke: " He'll be punished enough if he stays here with me. I have ways of punishing boys that would make yours look like fool's play! " Looking in Danny's direction, she almost smiled. " He's a big boy to carry, Captain, and you've no time to lose." She

walked across the room, picked up a poker at the fireplace, and started nudging Danny with it. " He's still
out like a light," she told them.

Captain Heath shrugged.

" Very well. We'll have to leave him here, I guess."

" Good," said Hannah, " now get going."

She picked up the candle and lighted their way to
the door. As they stepped across the threshold, the dog
began to bark again, and Danny heard Hannah say
soothingly: " It's all right, Prince. Be quiet! "

Danny let a long-drawn sigh escape from his lips. It
was a good thing to know the soldiers had gone. But
what would Hannah try to do to him now? She was a
big and able woman. He must be very wary.

She came back in and closed the door, then after a
moment she latched it. Leaning against it as though
she were tired, she stared across the room at Danny.
Suddenly a strange thing happened. She no longer
looked like a woman hard and capable and mean. Still
watching the boy on the floor, tenderness came into
her eyes, and she suddenly reached out her hand.

" Danny! " Very softly she called his name.

He groaned a little, then half turned, and she
crossed the room to him quickly. Kneeling beside him,
she spoke again.

" Do not be afraid, boy. Things here in this cabin
are not what they seem. If you are able to stand, please
do. I will take care of your bruises while we talk —
there is so much we must talk about — and at once! "

There was an almost desperate light in her eyes as
Danny half staggered to his feet. She, as well as he,

seemed thankful that no bones appeared to be broken, that he could stand almost erect, that most of his bruises were about his neck and shoulders.

" Hannah," he started to say, almost gratefully.

She too stood up and smoothed his hair back from his forehead.

" There's one nasty wound up here," she said. " Sit down on that chair over there, and I'll make a cold compress to cut down the swelling."

Now that he was up, Danny felt infinitely better. There were no soldiers to strike him with a musket, and whatever Hannah was trying to do he could not mistake her sincerity. While she dipped white cloths into a bucket of water on a shelf, she looked back at him, almost pleadingly.

" Get your senses together, Danny. There's so much for you to do! "

Suddenly Danny grinned, meanwhile rubbing his shoulder.

" I'm battered and bruised but I feel all right now. I can't say though that I don't understand — "

" Sit down on that chair," she commanded, " and I'll talk while I take care of you." Crossing the chair to him, she paused. " How old are you, Danny? " she asked.

" Almost fourteen," he answered, surprised.

" Almost fourteen," she repeated, " but if I don't miss my guess, you've a man's head on your shoulders. Now listen, Danny, and believe." Suddenly she stood up straight and taut. " I am *not* a Tory, or a Tory witch, as some people called me. I am as strong a rebel as you are — and I work for General Clinton as a spy up in these mountains! "

A spy for General Clinton! Danny could scarcely believe what he had heard, then he remembered how she had substituted a map for the one she had under the tablecloth.

" Believe me, Danny! You must believe me," she said tensely, " because it's only if you believe that I can trust you with a mission."

" A — a mission? " repeated Danny. " Oh, Hannah, I do believe you! I do! "

Suddenly she was crafty.

" What makes you believe me," she asked sharply, " after all that has happened here tonight? Surely you must have been convinced that Hannah's Rock is a Tory outpost! "

Danny looked serious.

" I believe you," he began, " because of one thing only. I saw you switching maps. You gave Captain Heath a different map from the one you studied together."

Hannah looked elated.

" I told you that you have a man's head on your shoulders. Now sit down there and let me bandage your head so you can make tracks back to the *Mollie-O*."

" The *Mollie-O!* " he echoed as he sat down on a chair and she began to apply cold compresses to his forehead.

" You'll have to reach it before sunrise," she told him, " or it will be attacked by Tories who will run it

aground at Esopus Island, near Kingston. They plan to
use the *Mollie-O* for a cargo boat."

" A cargo boat! " repeated Danny.

" That's what I said. The Tory plan is this. Listen
carefully now so you can tell all this to Mollie."

So Danny listened to the Tory plans. The map she
had given the soldiers, Hannah explained to him first,
would lead them straight to General Clinton who
would bring them to trial for their plot to burn the
white-pine forest. They could be imprisoned or they
could even be shot. And the *Mollie-O* must be warned,
she went on, because the Tories expected to use her to
carry white-pine trunks down-river to British-occupied
waters. The Tories planned to go aboard at Kingston
and once they had set foot on deck they would take her
over. Danny's message to Mollie must be: Don't put in
port at Kingston!

In less than a half hour, Danny was rowing away.
Hannah's words were like a battle cry ringing in his
ears. Don't put in port at Kingston! She seemed as
much of a heroine as Joan of Arc of France! To think
that she lived alone on that rock — known only as
Hannah's Rock to the British — and from her intelli-
gent maneuverings came plots and counterplots of in-
estimable value to the valiant American Army! She
was risking her life fighting for freedom just as they
were.

If only the *Mollie-O* were still anchored where he
had left her to follow mysterious moving lights! If
only Old Beaver hadn't decided to go on to Kingston
without him, hoping to contact authorities there! The

moon slipped down behind a mountain like a silver coin into a pocket. All was dark on the river now — the deep dark of the sky just before dawn. Danny knew he was headed northward in the right direction and he was not afraid. Not afraid until —

He thought he heard the sound of oars breaking water from a boat not his own. Was he being followed? he asked himself in panic. He could only hear — not see — but his hearing was acute. Drip. Drip. Drip! Surely there was a boat behind him. Indians, perhaps? Or the Tories already making for the *Mollie-O?*

Suddenly he heard, almost like a whisper, across a little space of water: " Danny! Danny! Where are you? "

Emalie! It was actually Emalie's voice like a sigh in the night. Then came another deeper one: " Danny! Danny! Are you on the river? "

That was Tad, he knew.

" Emalie! Tad! " he cried aloud. " I'm here! Here! "

An ecstatic sound came leaping back to him from Emalie's lips. " Can't you see us, Danny? Look! "

" See? " he mocked. " Can you see in the dark? "

Presently he realized he had turned a bend in the river and suddenly he saw a lantern hanging on a rowboat. There they were, Emalie and Tad, but there was another boy too! Who could it be and how did it come they were out here searching for him? Then ahead he saw the anchor lights of the *Mollie-O!* They had just begun their search, he surmised, but Emalie was calling: " Follow our light, Danny! Follow our light! "

Danny kept rowing and following the light as

though it were a guiding star! In no time at all, it seemed, they had reached the *Mollie-O,* and as he rowed up beside them, he saw the other boy was Rob!

" Yo ho, Danny! " Rob greeted him with the words they had always used back at Widow Reeves's."

" Rob! " Danny was so surprised that he could say no more.

They were already maneuvering their rowboat so that they could shinny up the rope ladder that hung amidships over the side of the *Mollie-O.*

" Hurry, Danny, come aboard, and tell us where you've been! " Emalie was calling like the magpie that she always was. " We want to tell you where Rob came from! "

" There's something Mollie must hear first," Danny
told them soberly as he pulled alongside their boat.

He realized as he climbed the ladder that Mollie,
with Old Beaver beside her, was waiting for him. He
heard a grateful voice call when she discovered him:
" It's Danny, Old Beaver! Praise be! "

When they reached the deck Mollie held out eager
arms to Danny.

" Sure an' it is one of the happiest moments I've
ever had to see that you are safe now! "

Danny drew away from her, troubled.

" But we're not safe, Mollie! We're not safe! "

" Speak, boy," she ordered, sensing his urgency.

He spoke very rapidly.

" I was kidnaped by the soldiers, Captain Heath
and one of his privates, and taken in a boat to what is
known as Hannah's Rock."

" Danny! " Mollie's sympathetic voice was a long, awed whisper.

" I'll tell you all about that later, but first of all you must know that the Tories plan to capture the *Mollie-O* at Kingston! "

" Capture the *Mollie-O!* " All on deck cried out.

Danny nodded his head.

" The Tories plan to use it as a cargo boat and make you take them back to British-occupied waters! "

Suddenly Old Beaver snorted.

"The *Mollie-O* a cargo boat! " He took his pipe out of his mouth and started for the helm. " We'll get our sails full, Danny, and we'll be passin' Kingston before the sun is up! "

So while the Tories waited to attack the *Mollie-O*, Danny was telling the story of Hannah and the trees that go to sea. Kingston was already behind them, and they were listening to him entranced. Even Rob took no time to tell that his father was hunting at Bear Mountain and he had rowed out to the *Mollie-O*, hoping to visit Danny.

But Danny was looking at Rob and saying, " You should have been with me at Hannah's Rock," which pleased Rob no end.

Mollie looked at the river. Presently she turned to Old Beaver and said, " Sure an' now is the time."

Old Beaver answered slyly, " Yes, now is the time."

Danny turned to face them.

" Time? " he asked, puzzled.

Old Beaver led him across the deck toward the helm of the *Mollie-O*.

" It's high time," he told Danny, " that you have the feel of a ship's wheel in your hand and begin to start mindin' the helm now that you've proved how smart you are."

" If you hadn't been smart," added Mollie, " the *Mollie-O* would have been captured and heaven only knows what would have happened to the lot of us."

Feeling the wheel of the *Mollie-O* under his hands, Danny looked out on the broad Hudson River as it lay before him. It has spoken to Danny just as Old Beaver had said it would. It would speak to him again and again as long as he was a river boy — through sunlight, through starlight, through moonlight — and most of all through the storms that lashed it from the high peaks of its mountains.

Biography of Olive Price

OLIVE PRICE was born in Pittsburgh, Pennsylvania. There she went to grammar and high school, and then to college at the University of Pittsburgh. There, too, she took her first job as advertising copy writer. Meanwhile, she hoped to do creative writing, and began writing plays for school production. Like all other writers, she chose New York as her mecca. At the age of eighteen she made a trip to New York that resulted in the publication of her first book of plays.

Miss Price has since written many other plays, some of which have been used on radio and television. In 1945, she began writing stories for young people. Her books have also been published in Denmark, Italy, and England. Several have been children's book club selections.

Her current book, RIVER BOY, has the Hudson River for a background during the stirring days of the American Revolution. It should be of special interest to boys and girls, for this river is rich in lore and legend.